THORAZINE BEACH

for my mother, Kathleen Eleanor Dain Harris,
and my father, Edmund Alexander Harris,
and my wife, Elizabeth Joan Deeley,
for creating homes built of love and books

Thorazine Beach

by Bradley Harris

winner of the 35th International
3-Day Novel Contest

anvil press • 2013

LIBRARY AND ARCHIVES CANADA CATALOGUING IN PUBLICATION

Harris, Bradley, 1952-, author
Thorazine Beach / Bradley Harris.

ISBN 978-1-927380-54-3 (pbk.)

I. Title.

PS8565.A64817T46 2013   C813'.54   C2013-904800-6

Cover design by Derek von Essen
Interior design by HeimatHouse
Author photo by Sandy Branson

Anvil Press gratefully acknowledges the support of the Government of Canada through the Canada Book Fund, the Canada Council for the Arts, and the Province of British Columbia through the British Columbia Arts Council and the Book Publishing Tax Credit.

Anvil Press Publishers
P.O. Box 3008, Main Post Office
Vancouver, B.C. Canada
V6B 3X5
www.anvilpress.com

Printed and bound in Canada

Children, we have it right here
It's the light in my eyes
It's perfection and grace
It's the smile on my face

Tonight when I chase the dragon
The water may change to cherry wine
And the silver will turn to gold

from *Time Out of Mind* (1980)
lyrics by Donald Fagen & Walter Becker

The governor of Tun-huang furnished us with all the provisions needed for crossing the desert. We then traveled on with the envoy of a camel train...In this desert are evil spirits and hot winds. Those who encounter them perish, to a man. There are neither birds above nor beasts below. Gazing on all sides, as far as the eye can reach...there is no guidance to be had, save the rotting bones of dead men, which point the way.

—Fa Hsien, AD 414

1.

Sometime in May...dusk
Summer Avenue—Memphis, Tennessee

I'm headed to my Thursday night Toastmasters club—the Delta Kings, a loopy little group with a green beans-and-cornbread, church hall sensibility I can't let go of. I'm on Summer Avenue, a couple of blocks shy of where it crosses Parkway and passes a long run of old houses, crossing Danny Thomas and into the hospital district. Six minutes, I'm thinking, to cut up to Jackson and along to the hall or I'm off the speakers' list. Then it occurs: This is the Delta Kings, for pity's sake. Green beans. Ham hocks. Kool-Aid in paper cups. They'll be fifteen minutes into the hour before the real meeting starts.

The limo-thing just ahead is pissing me off. It's huge, and black. The car looks like it's not only been lengthened but, oddly, widened, too. And old. A sixty-nine-ish, Lincoln-ish look. But all that's masked somehow under what looks like extra thick, bulging body panels and—then I see it. Thick, dark windows. Massive. Bulletproof glass.

I change lanes, commit to a right turn on Meyer, and the limo cuts in ahead. Shit. Slow. Like it's cruising. Middle of the road. And I can't get by.

The limo slows even more. Crawls. Ramshackle shotgun

houses. An empty lot. Then: a fierce, black wrought-iron fence, more than man-high, each vertical pale ending in a fluted African spear-point. A high-and-tight, golf-course lawn slides up the side of a deliberate embankment, a stepped sidewalk running up the middle. A dozen fonts, fountains, statues, scattered, no particular focus. Faux-Roman, faux-Greek, faux-tasteful. And the house: ridiculously new, comically massive for this neighbourhood. An absurd mix of brick, shiplap, plantation columns, and massive Teutonic oak doors—an evident Po-Mo joke played by some local architect upon someone with more money than art-historical savvy.

Sudden thought: I know whose car this is. The vanity plate: godsown. Martavius Something. I forget the last name. He did, too, a few years back, when he decided he should be addressed as His Eminence. COGIC, Memphis's own Church of God in Christ, had spun him out the door as soon as he'd begun preaching in one of their churches that one should, as a matter of protocol, bow to a minister. COGIC itself leans to the grandiose, to begin with. Going to church, for them, means twelve-button Steve Harvey suits, glittering dresses from the Diana Ross collection, some enlarged far beyond Diana's domain, and massive geometric sequin hats that might have been designed for the Queen of Hearts. What do you do when you're kicked out of a church? In Memphis, the answer is: Start your own, and go one better than the bunch who dumped you.

The limo stops. Middle of the street. Doors. One half of The Supremes steps out. Then the other. Heels. Sequins. Balancing huge hats. They stand, either side of the door, one holding it open. Respectful pause. Then…His Eminence.

Brushes a lapel. Reaches a hand into the limo.

The other two are busty, brown, statuesque. Now stepping out, under a hastily thrown-over coat, this third one is in something *clinging, gold, metallic. She is vaguely Asian. A confection. Tiny. A toy.*

The door shuts. The limo lurches.

The gleaming quartet starts up the steps toward the house.

His Eminence takes the rear, herding them up the walk. Turns. Smiles. An astringent stare at me. Turns away.

2.

"Shut up, Jack. You talk too much. Whaddaya want?"

Doubtless that phrasing isn't actually *in* the Starbucks barista training manual. But Nikki Jenks had long since written her own instructions, grown her own style. What's more, people not only put up with it, they liked it. Some of the regulars did, anyway. Guys, especially. *Beat me, baby, make me write bad cheques.*

Nikki wasn't the manager—just a shift supervisor. But she'd outlived, outdone, and done in at least three managers in the four years I'd been coming to the Summer Avenue 'Bucks. I knew why I liked her. She wasn't what you'd call pretty. Cute might be a stretch. But Nikki has…forget it—it's got no easy name. A smile, an evil wee twinkle, and an always-evident edge you could bleed to death on. And for all that, as Eliot put it, her laughter "tinkled among the teacups." She'd known that line when I'd first quoted it to her. Knew Milton inside out, and a good smattering of everything from Beowulf to Don DeLillo. She'd been an undergrad in English Lit at Memphis State, she told me, her twenty-something to my noticeably over-forty, around the time I'd been there for grad school, in the nineties. I hadn't known her in those days, it turned out, didn't even recognize her. But she'd known who I was. And that's the way she'd kept it since I'd first popped up at Nikki's 'Bucks.

"You people sell coffee?" I ventured. I felt a little like playing today. There was no lineup inside, just a couple of cars at the window, those looked after by some new kid.

"Hell, no," Nikki said. "We just sell that mocha-chicka-choco-chino crap. You want some of that?"

"Caramel macchiato with a shot?" I said, feeling a touch of surprise at my voice's rising, question-style. Might as well have been a question—you could *ask* for anything you wanted, but what you'd get was pretty much up to Nikki.

"Okay," she said. "But skinny for you, today. You been packin' it on there lately, Poncho."

"Twist that knife," I said.

"You love it, honey."

"Yep." I rolled my eyes. "And remember, I don't like foam."

Fssshht. Hiss. Gurgle. Clank of spoon on counter.

"Licked it off myself, Jack," she said, turning to set the cup down. "That'll be thirty-eight dollars."

"Is it *burned* coffee, Nikki?"

"Course it's burnt, Jack—you didn't read the big green sign when you pulled in here? Chick with the wavy hair?"

"I'll give you a five," I said, handing her the bill. "You can keep the change."

"Like I wasn't gonna." She rolled her eyes, tossed me a wink.

Inside, business was slow, even for the slowest 'Bucks in town. I looked around—I was all the business they had at the moment, in fact. I sipped as I stood at the counter, Nikki wiping and fiddling. "You this rude to *all* your customers?"

"Certainly not," she said without looking up. "They won't pay as much as you do, so you're gettin' the primo."

"Privileged, then."

"Quite," she said.

I looked about once more.

"Jack, your usual seat's available. Why don't you grab a *Wall Street Journal* and fake it for a while." Nikki's typical way of hinting she was busy. Or didn't want to talk. This one stung, though. There had been a time—Lynette's time—when I could look up something in the Dow, the Toronto, or the NASDAQ, even the Nikkei, and it would have been legit. All that, it was gone, now. And Nikki didn't know that history—so cut her some slack, Jack. Or did she know?

I turned to the rack. I actually did feel like having a look at a paper, a local one. But as close as you can get to a newspaper in Memphis is the *Commercial Appeal*. I'd sometimes sneak one to my table without paying, Nikki would pretend not to see, I'd pretend to be absent-minded, and one of the two would always work. "Just don't wrinkle it before you put it back," she said, *sotto voce*, and I whispered something to her. "And no coffee rings this time," she added.

A glance at the front page said all I needed to know. City school's security guy takes a dive for sexting a fifteen-year-old girl. City councilman's third DUI. City ranked ninety-fourth among nation's top hundred cities for public safety, places second in homicides per capita. City's downtown revitalization losing vitality. City becomes major centre for human trafficking. Shipments of Mexican drugs. Shipments of Mexicans. Meth lab in a junior high school boiler room, janitor and assistant principal arrested. God, I love this burg. I tossed the paper back on the rack. Nikki wasn't even at the counter, but from somewhere I heard, "Good boy, Jack." Patronizing as hell. But better than the usual, "Cheap bastard."

Why Starbucks had even *thought* about a store on Summer Avenue was beyond reason. Bubba don't do decaf cappuccino. And Summer Avenue is *all* Bubba country—Mexican incursions excepted—from its in-town beginning just a block east of the zoo and Rhodes College, out past the last, lone Assembly of God and into the land of cotton, soybeans, and tumbledown, wood-frame, septic tank acreages where the road starts to call itself Highway 70 for real. The beginning of Summer Avenue wasn't a *bad* part of town, exactly. You could send your kids to Rhodes for a couple of semesters, let them pretend, amid the old-South white columns, like they're going to Vanderbilt—*if* you had 30K searing a white-hot hole in your pocket. Or for twelve and a half bucks, you could hit the zoo on a summer afternoon and see what it is polar bears do when the heat gets up to one-oh-something, relative humidity hovering on the wrong side of a hundred per cent.

But cross the Parkway going east, and you'd start into Summer Avenue proper, the part I know. The Paris Cinema, where the movies they show aren't exactly, well, *cinema*. Or Parisian. A couple of self-styled "antique malls" whose merchandise might better be described as *debris*. A whole lot of stops aimed at those for whom booze, tattoos, and cheap cigs are regular offerings on the altar of existence. Evident rises and falls in fortune along the way. A decent Chinese buffet here, there a strip of long-lost glass-and-aluminum storefronts, cardboard for lease signs in the windows, faded and curled up to die. And right here, a block east of Berclair Baptist, at Summer and Stephens Station, a bright green Starbucks, plopped on a streetward outparcel of a half-empty, sixties-style shopping mall, looking desperately out of place, like an Armani suit in a bowling alley.

Word on the street is, some 'Bucks exec had gone wildcat a few years back, bought into this sure-fire, glow-in-the-dark development deal, signed too soon, requisitioned some pretty big company cheques, all without running it past their real estate people. The deal went south about fifteen minutes later. The exec was gone in a jiff, but just before the Starbucks board iced his last latte, they discovered he hadn't so much as read the lease he'd signed. Twenty years, damn near unbreakable, no sublet, and with enough penalty clauses and liquidated damages they figured that actually running a barely break-even store, though hopelessly misplaced, was cheaper than any way they could see of getting out. Even their own lawyers and financial people said so. Hence this go-through-the-motions farce, casting biscotti before the biscuits-and-gravy crowd.

I'd brought files and my laptop today. Took a few minutes out, my usual warm-up, to check my stamp bids on eBay. I'm a serious, geek collector—Canada bill stamps, used on promissory notes, 1864 to 1882. How's that for narrow? A few little five-dollar items. But I'd missed the big one—a first-issue eight-cent feather-in-the-bun, mint, fine to very fine centering, original gum, hinge remnants. Plus, I had legitimate stuff to do. As in: actual work. An expense claim I had to submit *today* or I wouldn't get paid at all, Eileen had told me (as always she told me, "for the last flaming time"). A quickie affidavit to draft on this unsuspectingly about-to-be-divorced guy holed up with the wrong woman at the Rebel Inn on Lamar—pics, digital recording, *Oh baby oh baby*, banging headboards, the whole nine yards. And a rather longer report I almost couldn't wait to write—*delicious* pics, video, but even better stills, in this insurance fraud case, Dwayne Poteat, the alleged paraplegic plaintiff hanging poised in mid-air, bum about two feet off the seat of a four-wheeler, over a dirt-hill jump just outside Dyersburg, an exquisite, wide-eyed grin smeared across his muddied face.

Starting to take a table, I stopped, decided on the big arm-chair in the corner, pulled down the sunshade. Overhead, high enough to discourage reaching, bolted to the wall, a single shelf. Books. Nearly all hardcover. Nikki's doing, I'd discovered the week before. "Gotta give the place a little tone, Jack." Her own books. A motley little clutch of them. *The Mill on the Floss*. *Lady Chatterley*. Locke's *Essay on Human Understanding*—the Nidditch edition, I noted. No slouch, our Nikki. A couple of Loren Eiseley's essay collections. A favourite poet—Jo McDougall's *The Woman in the Next Booth*. Armistead Maupin. Tama Janowitz—*Slaves of New York*. A *Moby-Dick* with a half-broken spine.

"Does anybody *get* that?" I asked Nikki. "Starbuck? First mate? Makes coffee on the ship?" Midtown, yes, Nikki told me, once in a while Germantown. Here, no. I smiled.

I looked at the lone paperback on the shelf, a dog-eared beater. Clifford Simak, *Way Station*. Golden age sci-fi. I'd first read it when I was fifteen and the world still held possibilities that didn't hurt or die or leave you behind, taking your heart. And here it was again, an intergalactic federation of a thousand intelligent species, a guy and a girl who held it all together. And a book that offered the best coffee in the galaxy, too, as judged by a friendly little blue guy, half a human tall—thanks, Cliff.

"*Way Station*'s a favourite of mine, too, Jack. Loved it all my life." Nikki smiled. I smiled back, sat, and sank into the book. I met again in its pages the aged mailman, the century-old dog, and the alien Ulysses, checked in a couple of E.T. diplomats from Lord knows where, and my cell rang. Must be Eileen, so I didn't even look. "Yes, Eileen, I know. I'll get it in today for sure—"

"Lucky you," the voice said, and I felt myself blush. MacDonald. First I'd heard from him in the couple of months since they'd promoted him to major, pulled him off the fraud squad and stuck him on that special task force, the whatever-it-was commission.

"You in your office?" he said.

"One of them," I said.

"Good," MacDonald said. "I'll be there in two minutes."

"But wait—I haven't told you which—"

"Two minutes," he said, and hung up.

3.

"She's a bit... *pissed*," Jackie, the receptionist, whispered.

From *way* down the hall: "I heard that!"

Jackie nodded, sending me behind her station and back. Fifty feet of hallway separated Eileen's inner office from Red Line's front door, but still she'd heard. I walked back, set my stuff on the floor beside her desk.

"I'm, like, fifteen minutes late," I objected. "You'd think it was a week."

"Time's money, Peanut," she said. "Park it."

I did. She sat, hands folded, an immaculately bare desktop.

"The dirty look," she went on, "is for all the times you *were* a week late. Whatcha got?"

"Well, first things first," I said. "Now, that divorce case—"

Eileen shook her head and smiled. "What *I* want to do comes first."

"That's *not* case files?"

"Case files are fun," she said. "Fun comes later. Paying you is not fun. Expenses first."

She began shuffling through the papers I handed her. Ticked a couple of items with a blue marker. Flipped pages. Then a circle, this time in red.

"What?" I said.

"Petro truckstop restaurant, West Memphis," she said.

"I was following this guy"—I held up the divorce file—"and I hadda go where he went."

"Granted," she said. "But did you really have to go for the all-you-can-eat chicken-fried steak extravaganza?"

"Yeah."

"Why?"

"Because it was a Friday, and Friday is chicken-fried steak. The all-you-can-eat meatloaf extravaganza is Tuesday."

"Have a salad next time." She gestured with the red pen. "Take it as personal advice." She grabbed a blue, ticked the item to say *okay*.

"Et tu, Brute?"

Good Christian woman, Eileen. And she can command a certain gentility on occasion. "As any Southern woman should," she'd say. But Eileen Leckie's also an ex-Bartlett cop. Twenty years on the force, she and her husband Les (gone these six years, now), before they started Red Line. The old cop in her can command attention, too, whenever she wants. And thus it came to be that, state-of-the-art intercom notwithstanding, the principal mode of inter-office communication at Red Line Investigations—with no clients present, at any rate—was shouting.

"JACKIE!"

"WHAT!"

"TWO EIGHTY-TWO SIXTY-THREE!"

"ROGER THAT!"

Faint giggles in the outer office.

Not that I minded the amounts of my expense cheques being known to the entire place. It's an investigations outfit—what *didn't* they know? I was rarely enough there, anyway—just when Eileen wanted me. And I wasn't, after all, an employee.

Red Line was the umptie-third agency I'd applied to, after the Garrison Security affair blew up, five-six years ago. Brilliant: I'd managed to bring down my own employer, second biggest security and investigations outfit in the region—not even so much knowingly, just tripped up in a tangle of goings-on in the vein of mail fraud and money-laundering and (just maybe) a murder mixed in there somewhere. Millions in assets seized. Licences jerked. A string of holding and operating companies ended up folded, spindled, and mutilated. Dozens suspected, eleven people charged, nine convicted. About eighty-five of Garrison's prize former-FBI agents thrown out of work, most with a measure of taint in the job market, even for those cleared in the investigations by the Memphis police, Tennessee Bureau of Investigation, and half a dozen lettered federal agencies. And every last one of those guys and a couple of gals, it seemed, harboured a resentment. All of it directed, in greater or lesser degree, at me.

Among those never indicted, never charged, never found: Isaac Breitzen, my old boss, the lord and master of Garrison's clutch of companies. A stand-up guy, early on, as Machiavellians go. Been a great place to work, people said, when his dad Buddy ran the company, when it was just the old, original security-guard outfit. Brown pants, yellow stripe, lunchpails. Regular folk. Friendly, and every employee, top to bottom, called him Buddy. Respectfully. But still, *Buddy*. The Breitzen I'd known was Ike, at first. Then *Mister* Breitzen, when Buddy took sick. Then, when Buddy was gone, Breitzen was simply *sir*—to everyone. Same tone as you'd address the queen's husband. By then, the job application form had grown to fifty-six pages— fifty longer than for my top secret clearance in the army—and even those of us already there had to fill it out. (Thank God the HR guy owed me a favour, let me fudge an answer or two.) Lie detector. Sworn oaths of allegiance—to the company, to *him*. Pat-downs in the front lobby, on a couple of days when Breitzen had felt the mantle of Roman senator especially heavy upon his shoulder.

Bars on the building, everywhere—even the windows of his eighth-storey office, where he'd had the fire escapes removed. He made all the staff memorize and recite, dead cold, his new, six-page, capital-C Code of Conduct, which he insisted be printed in red italics, a quirky font ripped from the Renaissance. Twenty-year guys, guys who wanted only to serve out their time walking security at strip malls, sitting night-shift desks in empty office buildings, guys who came to work on time and never took a sick day, guys who hadn't memorized anything since *Jesus loves me*, lost their jobs, no notice, no pay in lieu—Tennessee is a "right to work" state, which means the very opposite of what the phrase implies—because their memories couldn't get them past the second paragraph.

Breitzen was a small man, and became smaller, we saw, as time wore on. A bantam rooster in elevator shoes. He had a platform built in his office so his desk would be raised a step above the chairs his visitors would sit in. Story goes, Jim Bork, the company planner, wanted him to see some office-layout drawings, decided he'd plop his chair right up there and sit beside old Ike to show him. End of the morning, Bork was gone. End of the afternoon: Carpenters cutting down the platform so it would fit just one desk, just one gigantic leather swivel chair. And just one ego.

Laughter in the hallways became, through the years, whispers, glances, looks over shoulders. The building itself felt soaked in sadness. You daren't quit—you couldn't, not without bad references, recriminations. The whole place was simply *waiting*. Some employees—the optimists, we called them—were clearly waiting for Breitzen to die. Some might have been waiting to die themselves.

Middle of the night—not coincidentally the date of the morning raid the feds and Memphis PD had planned: Limo, private jet out of the Olive Branch airport, false flight plan filed. He took, they said, two suitcases, a couple of hundred pounds of hundred-dollar bills, a lifetime supply of Cuban cigars, and several custom crates bearing his precious collection of the drawings of Edvard Munch. Guys in black suits, briefcases full of platinum bars, palladium bars—silver and gold being, in Breitzen's world, distinctly lowbrow. The guys in suits didn't get to go, though their briefcases did. Those left behind, in the office or on the runway, all, in their own ways, screamed, sure as Munch's figure on the bridge. Where Breitzen is, they say, is a warm place. Certainly we all hoped it was.

Eleven *weeks* I was a witness, all added together. Investigation rooms, discoveries, and five courtroom trials—two criminal, three civil. All said and done, I was extruded out the bum end of the legal process with no job, no prospects, few friends, my distinctly unflattering picture in the paper, and little enough coin that I had to cadge my walking-around money off Lynette. Thankfully, no charges. But this last benefit, I'd finally come to grasp, was largely due to the all-too-apparent fact the trial judges and the D.A. both regarded me as too ineffectual, too just plain obtuse, to have had a knowing, causal hand in all this chicanery.

I'd managed to recover my P.I. licence. Barely. But you can't operate as a P.I. in Tennessee unless your *individual* licence hangs under the umbrella of an *agency* licence. The state government had long since said *okay* to my individual, but *no* to my getting my own shingle. They'd issue the individual when I'd found an agency home. I'd actually filed an administrative appeal, gone to Nashville for a hearing on getting my own company licence. I winced at the words. *Not anytime soon, Mr. Min-yard. Too many unanswered questions.* Hence my hoofing the whole city—and a few outlying burgs, too—looking for something, anything, in the investigations line.

I'd actually begun going back to freelance editing. Theses and dissertations, mostly. Tenure-hunting Memphis State assistant profs scrambling to squirt journal articles out of unreadable, turgid dissertations. *The* and *an* and *a* for Tamil- and Hindi-speaking engineers who thought their English was *almost* good enough. Verb tenses for work-all-night lab scientists from cold northern Chinese cities, smart enough to know their English blew. And from a Princeton business PhD, the most exacerbating case of gratuitous philological exhibitionism I'd ever seen. At first, all that wordsmithing was just to keep my hand in—we had more than enough money, on the home front, to ensure I needn't worry about that.

Then there was the call from Lynette. That night we'd be dining out, she'd told me. Restaurant, reservation time, separate cars. There'd been in recent weeks, maybe months, a little…*distance*, for lack of a better word. The trial. A certain…*fatigue*. Not to mention Lynette's travelling—rather more travelling than usual, of late, rather farther afield. And there were, as Lynette put it, "some things" she'd "heard," arising out of the Garrison affair and its admittedly embarrassing aftermath. Lynette, I knew, had lost real estate business over it. But still, we had…

I was halfway through a middlingly enthusiastic blackberry cheesecake when she bit the matter off. I felt the heat of shock on my own face. A half-assed protest. "No, Jack. You don't understand. I *have* left." No, Jack, you haven't "done anything wrong." No, we couldn't "talk," there'd be no "working it out." The house? "Sold," she said. "You'll need to be out by the eighteenth." But, Lynette, where will you…? "Out of the country," she said. That and "Martinique" and, more quietly, "I've met someone." Then a sudden reach across the table and, so very, very oddly, she kissed my hand, set it back down, wiped her mouth on a clean napkin. Rose. Left. And that was that.

That and the twenty K—now nearly gone—she'd dumped into my account a week later from some bank in the Cayman Islands. Was it given out of guilt? I never knew her motivation. But I'd spent all but a bit of the money.

"Earth to Jack…"

"Sorry, Eileen."

I looked up. She smiled again—this time a warm one, stripped of any sarcastic edge.

"I'm sorry, Eileen, I was just—"

"I know where you were, Jack." That smile again, a softer voice, and sad eyes.

Then a rather deliberate-looking perk-up. She leaned in. Grinned. "Whatcha got that's juicy?"

Eileen liked the divorce case report. Laughed at a couple of lines. (Couldn't resist, I told her—English major, you know.) "Good enough evidence for trial?" I asked her.

"Never gonna go to trial," she said. "Wife just wants her suspicions confirmed. Said she'd take my word for it, didn't even want to see the evidence. Now what about the insurance thing?"

I sat back. "You got a sense of humour today, Eileen?"

"It's Friday afternoon. Why not?"

"Then you might appreciate this," I said, reaching for a parcel I'd brought in with my files, the parcel neatly wrapped in brown paper.

Eileen gave it a querulous look and a grin. "You open it," I said. She did, and laughed out loud.

"My fifteen minutes of boss-annoying lateness," I said, "was owing to my needing to stop in for the frame."

"You know my tastes in art *very* well, Jack Minyard."

"EVERYBODY!" she shouted. "Get in here!"

They did, and a dozen women dressed in everything from smartly tailored suits to Wal-Mart sweats sat on chairs and table-corners or leaned, arms folded, against walls, and listened with smiles and laughs as Eileen told the story. *Weeks* on this investigation. Said the insurance company "just knew" the guy was a fraud artist, though the doctors hadn't caught him. I'd watched him for weeks, shadowed him as he went for this discovery, that doctor visit, physical therapy. Perfect perfect perfect—a wheelchair every time, helped into the car and out, the aching slowness, all the right moves and grimaces. All the right failures to grimace, too—this was neurological, after all, and there are some things you just don't feel, if the nerves are gone. The totality of evidence—a rapidly building mound of evidence—pointed in the direction that Dwayne Poteat was legit, the forklift accident had left his bottom half paralyzed, and everything I was gathering was making things *worse* for our case. Sure thing for a big six-digit lump-sum payout, or seven digits in structured settlement. Dwayne's attorney was going for the lump. But now…the picture was a coup. The picture would do it. Giant Bloodsucking Insurance Group of America would be, Eileen told me, *very* happy indeed.

I'd blown up my best shot to eleven-fourteen, had it put in an eighteen by twenty-four frame. Eileen kept the picture to her chest, didn't show the girls till she told how I'd noticed a four-wheel in Poteat's back yard one day, missing the next, back the day after. I'd managed to cash in a favour with a sweet girl at Dwayne's bank. Decently, mind you—she was married, Baptist, two-point-four children, what can you do? Thanks to her, I'd seen credit card charges, not Poteat's own but let's say "connected," up Dyersburg way. Too far out of Memphis for anyone to follow, he'd probably figured. And surely *one* indulgence of an old hobby couldn't hurt—hell, I could *feel* the guy's own rationale. Eileen turned the framed picture around and showed it. Dwayne Poteat's idiot leer, larger and wider than in the file photos—funnier, too—got them all on their feet applauding. "You go, Jack!" A couple of whistles, even.

Eileen, the last card I held, had outright declined to hire me back when, desperate as I was. Said she simply wouldn't have me as an employee, that I'd be "an occasional agent," with Red Line, sometimes Eileen herself, as my client, even though she'd set it up so my licence came under her aegis. No, she said, I was to do those sorts of things—"tacky" things, she'd said—that she wouldn't ask her employees to do. They were an office bunch, mostly—employment drug screenings, credit checks, background checks for everything from drug company vice-presidents down to Kroger bagging boys. Me—I was to do what they, Eileen's "own people," wouldn't do, shouldn't do, in Eileen's conception of the world. Anything that might get dirt on your shoes, dirt on your reputation, dirt in your mind, anything that might make you trip in the dark or even see something unseemly—that was where I'd come in. It meant a certain distance, a certain un-belonging, between me and Red Line.

But today I felt twelve feet tall, heard a couple of dozen iterations of *Way to go, Right on.* Today, I belonged. A cheque, albeit a small one, and the promise of more in the next week or two or three. I met the new girl, the shy one. Verlie. Averted eyes. A stutter. But something sparkled there.

Met the one guy, Tommy, new, the geek, the IT man—the only male employee I'd ever seen working at Eileen's. Nice guy. Took an interest. He asked me a couple of questions about what it's like to be a detective. "Private investigator," I corrected. "Only the police get to be detectives." A certain admiration, on his part, I thought. I Barney-Fyfed my way through a couple of answers, beyond what he'd asked, till his smile began to wane and it looked like he wanted to get back to work. Or back to some-thing.

The crowd thinned. Eileen took a call, waved us all out of her office. On the way from the stationery closet to her desk, Jackie even hugged me. Verlie offered me some homemade peanut brittle, and Christy bagged me a coke from the break room. More smiles, congrats, but quieter, now.

"Who's up for a drink?" I asked. "Dinner? Thought I might hit the Hunan Grill. The works. Anyone? My treat."

The ones with husbands and kids offered those by way of ex-cuse. The ones without looked at watches, busied themselves with purses, with papers on desks, a couple with *nothing* on desks.

There would be no takers tonight.

"All right, then," I said, trying for cheeriness. "Thanks, y'all." I never have been able to manage a convincing *y'all*. After nine-teen years here, I'm still too damn Canuck.

As I passed her desk, Jackie looked up. Smiled faintly, looked me in the eye, looked away, back briefly again. "Jack, you take care, now. *Good* care. Some Friday night, you and I, we'll…"

"Sure," I said. "Love to. We'll…"

"Absolutely. We will."

Years ago, it was, that I'd first heard that from Jackie.

"You have yourself a good weekend, now," one of us said.

"You, too," said the other.

I forget which.

The bell on the office front door. Their voices disappearing as the door closed behind me. The heat and noise of Summer Avenue.

4.

16 or 17 July, p.m., Late Afternoon or Evening
Queen Size Bed, Over Near the Right-Hand Side

I could *hear* it flip. The room was. That. Quiet.

It's an old alarm clock—eighties, I think. One of those kinds that displays digitally, but not with an LED-thingie or any of that. It was mechanical, a rolodex kind of thing. And, every minute, the number would flip. Voila! New number. I was keeping meticulous track of the minutes—thirteen…fourteen…fifteen…sixteen. But not at all of the hours.

Fascinating. Listen closely enough, and you could *hear* that flip. Was it really louder than my breathing?

The TV was on. Always was. What, I couldn't tell, else I'd have known the time. I'd turned down the sound, all the way, to listen. I was looking at the ceiling, at that dead, black, legged beast inside the glass globe of the room light. It sickened me, that dark, horrid thing, the very notion of it, though I never knew what it was. All I saw of the TV was flickering blue light, bouncing off the walls. Plato's cave, featuring Oprah, the five o'clock news, *Jeopardy*, *American Dad*, *Family Guy*, all in a reflected blur.

I fumbled left of me, on the bed, to find the remote. There.

No. That was my pills. Thorazine. Three left, I think. *This will even you out, Jack*, the shrink had said. Would I go to AA tonight? Maybe not. Maybe I'd missed already. Not much turned on it.

Hadn't I planned to play with stamps tonight? Today? Whatever time it was. I enjoyed slipping them lovingly inside the stock sheets. And there they'd stay. Reliable. Constant. Always there for you. They'd never drift, though I often did.

I was here in Memphis—that much I knew—and lying on a bed. Except I was lying on a chaise longue. A motel in Penticton, peach country, years and years ago, but still so bright. Lying on the motel's own beach. Slightly off-season. Warm, not hot. The occasional boat, the occasional splash in the water, a jump off the floating raft. Quiet. With—who had it been? Gina, surely. I couldn't quite *see* her.

But there she was, her own chaise longue beside mine, a table in between for drinks, hats, sunscreen, motel room key. *Our* room. Her car. *Our* weekend. Gina or whoever—Gina, surely— was reading a P.D. James, I think. And I had *Day of the Triffids* and an issue of *Sky and Telescope*, and kept switching between. We were right on the beach, had moved our seats and things just a spit away from the little, lapping waves at the lake's edge. Something dark, human-sized, moved by in the water. I would look up at her, say *Hey—did you know…?* She would look up, say *Listen to this, it's funny…* We'd look up, sometimes, and just smile.

Three days there, I remember, exactly. Three or four. And each day lasted, like…a whole *day*.

We were lying there. And these three days were the only part of our year and some together that wasn't, for me, about *getting* Gina, wasn't about *losing* Gina.

5.

Two minutes became twenty, twenty-five. I'd already moved to a table, set up my laptop and started on my reports. Typical MacDonald. He'll knock on your door to the pico-second, given a timed party invitation, before you're even ready. And he'll turn up unannounced, anytime and anywhere he pleases. Crime scene—johnny on the spot. But make an *appointment* with the bugger…

I presumed the SUV that pulled in was MacDonald. He'd bought a brand new car, I guessed. A big Cadillac Escalade—certainly showy enough for Mac. Black, freshly washed and waxed. No, I realized—an ultra-dark purple. Custom paint job, no doubt. The Escalade parked facing the street, its back to me. The occupant—tinted windows, I couldn't see clearly—looked in the rearview mirror, looked again, backed out, turned right, and left the lot.

I'd got half-interested in some half-assed talk he'd been engaging in lately. Some commission thing. Memphis PD had commissions, studies, and task forces on bloody near everything. No small number were inward-looking, ultra-sensitive things. There'd been one on cops' involvement in drug transactions—stuff disappearing from the evidence lockup, finding its way back into the hood. And another when, under the reign of the previous mayor, King Willie, the lieutenant in charge of the mayor's bodyguard found with bundles of drug money stashed in the rafters of her garage.

Then there was the "new commission." That's all the name MacDonald had ever given it, though a couple of times he'd said "task force." He's a passive-aggressive conversationalist, is our Mac. Half the time tells more than he knows, half the time less. Plays his cards close to the chest, then lays them down face up when he goes to the can. He'd been alternately withholding and leaking vague stuff about "import-export," a coy reference here and there to "cargo" that I somehow knew wasn't about plastic Hello Kitty purses or illegal knock-off cell phones. I knew better than to dig—he'd tell me when he needed to. Or wanted to. Or painted himself into a corner and had no other choice.

Then, a few minutes and half a hastily scrawled report later, I saw him. *Heard* him. He turned off the ignition, but the engine had other ideas, ran on a good thirty seconds. MacDonald ignored the splutter and walked right in like he owned the place. How he makes a dress shirt stay crisp in hundred-degree temperatures is beyond me, but he does it. The man's a clothes-horse. He said he'd just ordered some tailor-made shirts from England, last I saw him. It was one of those he was sporting now, I guessed. A loud, blue- and scarlet-striped, British-exec kind of thing, with an equally loud lemon-yellow tie that didn't *quite* go, but somehow was perfect. He sat.

I had to disparage him for something. "What's with the wreck, Mac?"

"I'm undercover," he said.

"As what?"

"As you, Jack. I asked the motor pool for the crummiest piece of shit they had."

"Not the most stylish of disguises. Or the most effective," I said as MacDonald waved a finger at Nikki, who seemed to know exactly what he wanted and tossed off a cheery *Yes, sir!*, actually blushing a little as he thanked her. "Or the most subtle."

"I'm sorry? What was that?" he said.

I pointed. "Lookie there. A white Crown Vic. Bad putty job on the doors. Numbers painted over—brush job, I note. Searchlight. Baby moons on all four wheels. And about twelve aerial holes. Nobody'd spot *you* for a cop trying not to be spotted for a cop."

"I thought the run-on engine would be a nice touch when I pull up at the doughnut shop, Jack. Leave them guessing—is he? . . . or isn't he?"

"Only his tailor knows for sure," I said.

"And yours?" MacDonald said, never skipping a beat. "The 'K-Mart refugee look' the in thing these days, among you upper middle-class white boys?"

"You've given up the pointy shoes and the Mister T starter set, I see, Mac. Out of fashion in the deep hood this year?"

He smiled at Nikki as he took the cup and saucer she had walked over for him. "Thank you, dear," he said, and began fiddling with the teabag string.

"'*Dear*'?" I said. "That's new. And what's with the teacup? Not Starbucks issue."

"Aynsley," he said. "Brought it in. They keep it for me, behind the counter. I'm going British, you know. Saville Row. Bespoke. I'll never buy anything off the peg again."

"Okay, Mac," I said. "We've traded enough abuse and one-up stuff. What up?"

"Something gotta be 'up' for me to want to see my old buddy?"

"Generally," I said.

"I'm hurt, Jack. Really, I am."

"Impossible," I said. "You're an insect. You have only the most rudimentary nervous system."

"True, dat." He sipped his tea, his pinky ever so slightly out. That, too, was new. And downright creepy, from a former vice cop.

"By the way, Mac," I said. "Congratulations. On your promotion, I mean."

"Thank you, Jack," he said. "It *has* been a long time coming. And it's all been a bit of a surprise."

Major is an unusual rank for a city police department to have on its roster. It all started when the MPD's union, ages ago, managed to put through a provision that handed a captaincy to any old patrolman who slugged it out thirty years without getting caught in any of the shenanigans too many Memphis cops get caught in. Legit captains didn't want to be mistaken for one of *those*, so the new rank of major was born, just for them. Now, they had lieutenants-colonel. Colonels, too. I expected to see a brigadier-general any day now, staff car, braided aide-de-camp, and all.

"Thought I might be getting a precinct," Mac said. "I was kind of hoping for Union Avenue—still inner-city enough for some action, but then you've got the cotton mansions on Belvedere, Bellevue, so forth, some good restaurants. Midtown. The arts. And a better class of person," he added.

"Time was, Mac, your idea of fine dining was pulled pork, beans, and a mess o' collard greens at Neely's barbecue."

"Tell you a secret, Jack?" He leaned in and whispered. "Still is. But I'm buckin' for the big time, and it behooves me to be seen in some fancier places."

"Oh, then the Union Avenue precinct would have been perfect," I said. "There's a Popeye's Chicken across the street."

"Racial profiling, Jack?"

"No. But it's a perfect profile of you."

"You wound me so." He leaned back, smiled, spilled a spot of tea on his tie—a screaming yellow silk, which he wiped fruitlessly with his napkin. "Damn! Now I know why you always wear those ugly brown paisley ties."

"Till they get too stiff with dried old gravy," I said.

"Shit," he said. "Don't s'pose these dry-clean very well, do they?" I shook my head. "Seventy-five bucks, this. So where do you get your ties, Jack?"

"eBay. Sixty-five, seventy-five cents. A buck, sometimes."

"Wow. Plus shipping, of course."

"Including shipping."

"Polyester?" he asked. "Recycled restaurant placemats?" He reached. Felt. "Damn! Silk!"

"And if I spill something, it's no big—"

"Which you *always* do, Jack."

"Only when I'm eating or drinking or doing something else. Anyway…silk. People's Republic of China. Most I ever paid was about three bucks. Lowest winning bid…the princely sum of six cents."

"So you're deliberately bypassing my people, the hard-working American black folk, ensconced against their wills in Dickensian factories, the dark, satanic mills, hunched over their work stations, hand-stitching neckties the good old American way? All in favour of buggering our trade balance with all those vile commie countries?"

"'Buggering'?" I said. "Another new one for you."

"Learned it from you, Jack. You Canucks and Brits have got better cussing than we Amurrikins do. I'm making a study of it."

"Good move," I said. "First met you, back in your patrol car days, about the best you could do at the time was 'muh-fuh.'"

"And high-quality invective it remains, Jack. For the right audience."

"Ever tasteful," I said. "Positively Shakespearean. Anyway… silk…China…cheap…"

"Speaking of which, Jack…"

"So you do want something."

"Naturally I *want* something, Jack. I admitted that right up front."

"You did not." I turned back to typing the next line of my report, looked at my watch. About two and a half hours to get to Office Max, print, stop at whozit's for that frame I wanted, and get to Eileen's office.

"Of course I didn't," said Mac. "Never admit to anything. Make them prove it."

"Well…?" I kept working.

"Speaking of export-import…"

"You going to get me in on another one of your multi-level marketing schemes, Mac?"

"I admit the water-purifier thing didn't pan—"

"Never admit anything," I said, still typing. "Get on with it."

"I need you to do some work. Work for me." He bent his head for eye contact. "Is all."

"Paid work, Mac? Or is this the local LEO cashing stamps for favours from his friend, the highly ingenious but down-on-his-luck private detective, like on TV?"

"Why, Jim Rockford, you nasty little man," Mac said. "I never indulge cliché."

"You grab a new cliché a week," I said. "You're hooked on cliché."

"I can quit anytime I want to."

"So quit now."

"Um…not *this* time, Jack, I'm afraid."

"Well, then I'll be ready to help *next* time."

"C'mon, Jack…"

His voice had changed. It was something like real pleading, now.

I looked up. "This to do with the new ... whatever-it-is commission?"

"Yes."

"Yes?"

"Yes and no."

"Always is, with you."

"It's ... private. Sort of."

"Who'd you boink this time, MacDonald? Did I perchance accidentally capture the action on film?"

"Not the places *you* go, Jack. The Rebel Inn? Jesus."

I looked him in the eye. "How'd you know I was there?"

"I drove by. Just ... happened."

"I thought *I* was the grand champeen of 'It just happened.'"

"The profession ... *you* know ... takes one anywhere."

"'One,' Mac? Another novel slice of lexical pretension," I said.

"One does one's best."

"Well, perhaps one could get on with whatever freebie fricking favour it is that one wants from one's—incidentally, rather neglected—friend."

"Here's the deal, Jack—"

"And, speaking of deals, one will be receiving some sort of compensation, I presume?"

"One will. I'm sure, I'm ... confident one will."

"To state the query with maximum directness and economy ... what?"

"I couldn't squeeze a dime out of the commission, Jack. Not for this."

"Didn't Chief Larry and Mayor Wharton dump in zillions?"

"Um ... yeah. Sure. But the task force mandate ..."

"I thought it was a 'commission.'"

"It's…complicated."

"Enlighten me."

"Well, the task force is part of the commission. Sort of."

"So who's on this task force?" I asked.

"Well, there's me."

"And…?"

"Um…*you*, Jack."

"So the official staffing of this task force is…one?"

"Um…slightly less, actually."

"Stands to reason," I said. "And I'll be paid in…Chinese food?"

"Probably some of that, yes. I think the task force could see its way clear to—"

"Gasoline?"

"Count on it. Don't know where I'll—but, yeah, count on it."

"Tailor-made British shirts, perhaps?"

He brightened at that. "Actually, given we get someone to take the measure of your…ample girth, perhaps we *could* arrange—"

"Impromptu dates with fabulous babes?"

"I'm not a miracle worker, Jack. And I wouldn't even know where to look for the types *you* go for."

"Educated? Erudite? Able to use 'postmodern' in a sentence? Given to witty, improvisational uses of excerpts from the later Wittgenstein?"

"*Those* I could find," he said. "It's the fifty-something bimbos in hoop earrings and lip gloss and spandex jeans I don't know."

"I'm looking for the whole package—all in one."

"Vassar by way of Vegas, as it were."

"Right."

"Good luck with that. Besides, man, you're *sixty*. Just about to turn, what, next couple of months, as I recall…?"

"MacDonald," I said. "There may be snow on the roof—"

"And not much of that."

"I've been striving for the Bruce Willis look."

"And when Bruce Willis gets to be a pasty-faced, old, fat, bald guy, you'll have it nailed."

"Have a little respect, MacDonald. *Today*," I said. "I turned sixty today."

"Many happy returns," he said.

"Not that *you'd* notice."

"I'm here, ain't I?"

I looked at my watch. "Yeah. You are."

"I even got you something for the occasion."

"What?"

"In my car. Gimme the keys to Mitzi and I'll move it from my car to yours."

"Why don't you just bring it in—"

MacDonald stood, shook his head. "Keys." Held out his hand.

I produced them. "Back to work," he said, his hand waving contemptuously. A minute later, I glanced up. MacDonald, darn near staggering under the weight of an enormous cardboard box. It wouldn't go in the trunk, I could see him judge. He did manage to get it into the back seat, with more than a little bashing and shoving.

Back inside, sweating, he loosened and pulled off his tie, which was now, beyond the tea stain, nastily soiled from his struggles outside. He loosened the top button of his shirt.

"Take it off, baby. Take it all off!" Nikki called from behind the counter.

"You wish!" MacDonald said, and tossed her the tie to throw out.

I thought I heard *I do* from Nikki's direction.

MacDonald turned to me, sat again.

"I appreciate the gift, Mac. What the hell is it?"

"For when you get home," he said.

"No, seriously, man. What—"

"It *is* a serious gift," he said.

He didn't smile. Didn't bristle. MacDonald reached inside the suit jacket he'd hung over one of the chairs, pulled out a notebook, bound with a rubber band. Looked around. Just one customer, way on the other side—the crazy Russian lady, always conducting an invisible string quartet.

"Something to do with those fabulous babes?" I asked. "Babe-in-a-box?"

He spoke quietly. "Funny you should put it that way."

6.

17 July, 2:20 p.m.
New Nam King Buffet

You could always get a seat—that was one virtue of the place. Shabby, but it was clean, in its way, the smells of bleach, ancient carpet, onions and curry mingling in an unholy olfactory union. And no one knew me here, among the customers at least.

Midway through the big bowl of chocolate pudding I was downing to celebrate my having been so good at confining myself to veggies, I felt a tickle in my pocket. Flipped my second-gen cell open—I'm not yet smart enough for a smart phone. Gave it my cheeriest "Good afternoon. Jack Minyard speaking." Lots of Toastmasterly vocal variety and bright cheer. For a while I'd been going with just a snapped *Minyard*, like TV detectives do. Then *Go for Jack*. Both, I'd suddenly realized, I'd picked up from MacDonald, which made me wince at their glibness. So back to the way Mom taught me.

"Jack…" the voice said slowly. A voice I recognized, but didn't. Female, fifty-something, I guessed. Question, hesitation hung there. Then: "Jack, I'm so…I just wanted to hear your…and wish you a happy birthday."

I smiled. Sat up straight. "Well, thank you so much, it's…umm, forgive my asking, but I'm not quite sure to whom I'm—"

Hesitation. Click. I looked, redialed. Nothing.

THORAZINE BEACH » **39**

My bill came. I looked up. The restaurant's front door squeaked open.

A nervous, balding little white guy in an expensive sport coat followed another man in. A man with no nervousness at all. Flamboyant. Gold watch, gold cuff links. And, I saw, a gold tooth. The man I knew as His Eminence.

I looked down at my bowl of chocolate pudding.

7.

17 July, 4:20 p.m.
Red Line Investigations — Eileen

I'd cheer myself up, right here in Eileen's parking lot, I thought, by finding out what MacDonald's gift was. It wouldn't be like peeking into presents before the party. What party? Besides, it wasn't wrapped—just whatever it was, crammed inside a huge cardboard crate that had seen a whole lot of handling. What little printing there was looked vaguely foreign—something about the fonts. Just numbers, that I could see, and two or three iterations of THIS SIDE UP. Gutsy cardboard—no tearing that by hand—stapled and riveted to a rough wooden crate-frame inside. A *clank* inside, a time or two. Heavy as hell, I noted, and heard myself grunt as I tried to shift it to see whether there was more writing on the side facing the rear of the back seats. A bitch.

"Evening, Jack," called a couple of the girls exiting Red Line. "Have a good one." I glanced. Waved and smiled—rather idiotically, I thought, my shirt front dirtied, now, and shirttail out, wiping my brow with that old towel from the back seat floor. What *was* that stain?

"Jack," the voice said. Startled. I hadn't heard Eileen come up behind me. I stood, turned.

She looked my disheveled figure up and down. Reached up, adjusted my tie. As if that helped. "Um, Jack?" she said quietly, looked away, looked me in the eye. "Will we, um, see you at church Sunday?"

"I guess," I said, breathing heavily.

"Good. Good," she said.

"Well. Sunday, then."

"Sunday," she said.

"Sunday it is. Guess I better…"

"You still going to the eight o'clock, Jack?"

Back when, Lynette and I had always gone to the ten-thirty service at Grace St. Luke's Episcopal. Choir. Kettle drums. A cornet, flute, maybe a French horn. Toney. Church for the well-heeled, the ten-thirty was. You could hear Paul's epistles read by a lector who just happened to be the city's number one neurosurgeon. Hear the week's announcements from a professor of opera. Take communion bread handed you by a real estate developer who owned half of Midtown. Lynette knew everyone. Everyone knew Lynette. Everyone *loved* Lynette. Everyone said hello to me.

I could let go of the people. It was the *place* I couldn't let go of. I hadn't met God in years, not since I'd got sober in AA. But I met him again, soon as we started going to Grace St. Luke's. Not in the music, mind you. Jesus, I hated those people who prattled on about the fricking music at the ten-thirty. *Oh, it's so LOVEly…It's the MUSIC I really come for, you know…* As if *that* wouldn't piss God off. And he and I got closer when I started coming earlier. No, in the quieter, stiffer eight o'clock service, I heard him in the spaces *between* people, *between* talking. In the space between a cough and a shuffling of feet. In the space between the rector's amen and the creaking of an oak pew-back. At the eight o'clock, they give you a dirty look if all you put in the collection is a couple of crumpled ones or, like Doreen, desperate and *believing*, hands held high in the front row, your tithe rattles in the brass plate. Communion is thinly populated at the eight o'clock. Near-silent. Solemn. I could hear my knees crack as I knelt. Whisper: *Body of Christ…bread of heaven*. I could *hear* the bread torn from the loaf, *hear* the saliva working in my own mouth as I took it. Whisper: *Blood of Christ…cup of salvation*. Drink, wipe, drink, wipe. And when the cup came to me, I would cross my arms—the sign of the cross of St. Andrew, I fancied—decline to drink, and rise to my feet. I wondered: Did the acolytes think this was rejection? Insubordination? Who were *they* to think such a thing? Each week, I resented that, just a little.

Hi, my name is Jack. I'm an alcoholic. Resentment is an art form, for us. We grow it, water it, cultivate it, like herbs on a kitchen windowsill. They had gluten-free wafers, for Christ's sake, if you wanted. But no grape juice for the alkies. Perhaps, they'd have me believe, I was the only one of *those* people among the saints—they'd go marching in, I'd go staggering by. No—couldn't be. Could I be the only alkie here? As others in the eight o'clock prayed about foreclosure and dead grandsons in Afghanistan and cancer and legs that no longer worked and brains unable to remember their own mothers and brothers, I prayed, sometimes, about that tiny, stupid resentment. Some day, some day. Jesus, please, some day.

"The eight o'clock," I answered Eileen. "Yes. The eight."

"Good. Good," she said again.

"Well…" Cough. "Eileen, I…"

"Yes, yes, of course."

"Was there…"

"…something…?" she filled in.

"Else?" I said.

A silence between.

"Jack?"

I simply looked at her.

"Jack, do you remember, um...?"

"Remember whom, Eileen?"

"'Whom.'" She chuckled. "Always the English major, Jack."

I kept looking at her.

She glanced away, as if unsure, then looked me square in the eye. "Um...Barbara Jean McCorkle?"

Memory flooded in. Lynette and I had known her during the earlier time we'd been going to Belleau Wood Baptist, out on Gee-Town Parkway. You couldn't *not* know Barbara Jean McCorkle. *Twenty-six thousand*, that congregation. Yet I swear you could hear her voice, see her face, right through the shoulder-to-shoulder crowds around the foyer coffee stands between Sunday school and service. Endless committees. Our dining room, furniture stacked high, stuffing envelopes. Party decorations. Box lunches for the homeless. And that *voice*. Toxic. Christ, the woman had a voice that could strip paint.

"Um, yeah. Sure. Nice woman."

"*Lovely* person."

"Yeah."

"She goes to your church now, Jack. Grace St. Luke's. The five o'clock, mind you."

"Belleau Wood's loss," I said, "is our—"

"Jack," she said, and let that hang a moment. So did I. "Jack, I've asked her to..."

"To what, Eileen?"

"Well...just to look you up. Look you up...is all."

"Wonderful," I said. "Just give me her e-mail, she and I'll have coffee sometime. Ooh! Look at the time, I—"

"Jack." Her head was cocked to one side. I knew that look.

"Jack what," I said flatly.

"Jack, we're ... we're all ... worried about you."

"I'm fine, I'm fine, Eileen."

"The weight you've put on, Jack. You're *sixty*, now."

"Thank you for remembering."

"It's not just that, it's ... "

"Look, Eileen, it's nothing I can't ... " I couldn't finish that sentence. And she didn't.

Eileen reached into the pocket of her jacket. Held out her fist, opened it, palm up. A prescription pill bottle. "You must have dropped it on my office floor."

"Oh, thanks, Eileen. My blood pressure medicine. Appreciate your rescuing that," I said, taking the bottle and tossing it through my car's open back door onto the front passenger seat. The tone of its rattle reminded me there were only a few pills left. "I've got to get a new prescription Monday. Visit good old Doctor Nigeria. Good guy, you know, he—"

"Jack, I know my medications pretty well. Les used to take more than a few."

"I take a few myself," I said, cranking out a chuckle that couldn't have sounded anything but hollow.

"Jack, it's Thorazine. It's not for blood pressure, it's—"

"Well, Doc Nigeria's got me on a complex of medications, actually. I've started a better diet—"

"Peanut brittle and Coca-Cola?" she intruded.

"You don't miss much, Eileen, do you?"

"Private investigator," she said. She smiled a little, this time.

"I know you'll be okay with the diet thing. You've done it before. Lynette told me you'd made it last *years*, once. And I know you'll like MacDonald's birthday present."

"Jesus, Eileen, you *know* what this thing is?"

She shrugged. "He stopped by this morning. We, um ... talked."

"Am I the *only* one on the outside, here?" I said.

"You might be," she said. "For now. MacDonald said your best bet might be to cut the cardboard with your crate still right in the car, take it inside in pieces, one by one."

"Why don't you just tell me, Eileen?"

"Oh, no. Couldn't possibly," she said, tossing in a little cheer. "MacDonald told me he wanted to drive you mental."

She blushed a bit when she heard what she'd said.

"Jack," she said. "Thorazine. I know what it's for."

My mind wandered to her office. Her and Les—a wedding picture. Her and Les—in a patrol cop's uniform. Her and Les— Grand Canyon. The Liberty Bell. Monument Valley. Point Reyes. With grandchildren, dogs. Arm in arm, on the beach at Destin, Florida. Six years, and those dozen or more pictures had never moved, except for dusting. Her eyes told me she did know what Thorazine was for.

I felt tears somewhere behind my eyes. I fumbled for words. "The Desipramine," I said. "It just never worked, whatever the dose they tried. Everything was so…so *grey*. Sunny day, and it felt like rain. I cried. I couldn't…I drank. I *drank*, for Christ's sake, Eileen. Eighteen years sober and I…I drank. Just one, just that one time, but—"

"Shhhh," she said, and she held me, just held me, for the longest time. We stood there in the parking lot, in mid-whatever, my car door open, my shirttail out, her purse dropped to the ground. I knew better than to speak, better than to *do* anything. I just let her hold me. And in between the car horns and the eighteen-wheelers' air brakes on Summer Avenue, I could hear her breathing.

8.

Treasure Fricking Island. 4720 Summer Avenue, right between the Imperial Lanes, west side (bowling, video games, light lunches, beer), and on the east, past a wild kudzu hedge that had grown up through a rusted chain-link fence, one of the most frequently robbed Bank of America branches in the country. Handy to the Mapco that carried my brand of cigarettes and the cheapest gas on Summer Avenue, a block along from a shabby little nameless beer joint with terry cloth tabletops where I'd made myself a regular in about three visits, over-tipping for endless refills of Diet Coke and occasional bags of Cheezies as I half-read a book, half-heard the bar-talk.

The Admiral Benbow Inn was the last local bastion of a fast-fading motel franchise chain that still hung on here and there in Alabama, Georgia, maybe northwest Florida. The Summer Avenue edition still looked a bit like a "family" motel, in a sixties kind of sense that had never been updated. Big-paned glass-windowed lobby. Stone-work walls, now much patched with the wrong kind of concrete. Cracked walks. Peeling paint over peeled paint. You could see a whole lot of used-to, at the Benbow. The restaurant that used to serve steak sandwiches to State Farm insurance and Ace Hardware store guys from the neighbourhood, bacon & eggs and bottomless cheery coffees to morning travelers about to get back on the road, whipped-cream pancakes for the kiddies. The restaurant still ran. Some days. Coffee and continental breakfast in the lobby, for overnight guests: Yesterday's urn, still plugged in, and a box of day-olds from Donald's Donuts down the street. The back room—a now-paintless wooden sign, over the door: The Admiral's Quarters—where the Rotary and the Lions used to meet. Now, a black church rented the room Sunday mornings, bass drum and a B-3 organ banging and raging, an over-wrought, sweaty preacher intoning from nine in the morning till noon, when Mrs. Patel would hammer loudly and shout, waving the paper contract, and say they had to get out. Once in a while you'd see some lost bunch slouching about of a weekend evening, guests at a forlorn wedding reception, standing around with cigarettes and rum-and-Cokes, wondering how in hell *their* friends could have seen fit to rent *this* dump. And about once a week, thanks to internet reservations and relaxed standards of truth in website photography, you'd see them arrive in the slanted sun and shadow of a late afternoon: Minivan, often as not. They could afford the Hampton Inn, but Dad, perhaps, had felt an urge to economize. Ward, June, and the Beav. Could hear them, too. *Come on, honey, it's just for one night…But, dear, the pictures, it's not at all like—…Hey, son, let's check out the pool …Good Lord, Howard, I don't like that green tinge…*

A hundred and sixteen-fifty a week. Cheaper if I'd pay ahead—five weeks for four. Mrs. Patel liked cash. Mrs. Patel liked inventing charges, too. For towels. Pillowcases, even. Toilet paper—dollar a roll if you didn't bring in your own. A surcharge for guests who wished to use the pool, which Mrs. Patel thought should be everyone. I escaped that, noting I, too, didn't like the green tinge. "It will be rectified, it will be rectified with utmost speed," Mrs. Patel assured. "I can't swim," I said. And then there was the "key fee." That I couldn't escape, but eventually the fee just disappeared—simply forgotten, I think. I presumed the absentee owners of this last-gasp franchise never knew about the extras.

Mine was a big room, no doubt. "Family," indeed. Two queen-size beds, and they came nowhere close to filling the place. Night tables, dresser, desk, all in a 1978-ish round-cornered, oak veneer, commercial grade style, all having seen their share of spilled drinks, kicks, and dragging things across the very outdoor looking indoor-outdoor carpet. A chair I had to ask to be replaced three times before getting one that didn't wobble precariously.

I'm not sure Mrs. Patel ever liked me, exactly. But over time, Mrs. Patel came to watch out for me, watch for whoever might slow or hesitate as they passed my door. I was, after all, as close to 'class' as the Benbow usually saw. "Thieves," Mrs. Patel said. "They are all thieves, I am telling you."

One afternoon, some guy knocked on my door. Through the peephole, I vaguely recognized him from a few doors down the wing. I answered, bare feet and jammy pants and T-shirt. "You use this?" he said. Sleepy, I said *Sure*, and he and his friend schlepped in an upholstered couch, somewhere in length between a loveseat and a full-size sofa, set it against the wall. "Um ...thank you," I said, vaguely. "No problem," they said, and left. A few days later, I found some crumpled papers lodged between the two cushions. An Aaron's Rental contract and a bill for a bunch of weeks unpaid. Great—I could now add receiving stolen property to my list of moral misdemeanors. *They are all thieves, I am telling you.*

Home. Four years. I knew no one by name, they didn't know me. Not, at least, past nodding mumbles in passing. *'Sup. Hotnuff foyah. Awright awright.*

There was that fifty-something guy in 103 who said he was running his eBay business out of the room. He might have been. There were boxes of *stuff* all over the place—you could see them, daytimes, through his always-open drapes. A computer. And he did take a small armload of packages to the post office every day. But he also watched an awful lot of daytime girl-TV, and rarely left the place, and he looked a lot to me like a guy in denial about a divorce, or a death. Till the day the maid screamed, the ambulance came, people stood around the door, gurney in, gurney out, and the ambulance drove away in silence—no speed, no siren, no pomp to mark the passing of that life.

There were those people who worked, left each day at regular times, returned. And those who stayed *all day* around the Benbow. What they did, I never knew. I do know I was more than once taken for a narc, more than once offered a flat-screen TV at a remarkable price, and one time, a dealer's box full of coins, stacked in individual 2x2s, priced for sale. "Getting rid of my collection," the guy said. A collection upon which he was devoid of numismatic knowledge.

And *just* once, a twenty-ish woman at my door, dressed in… I wasn't quite sure, but it was *very* skimpy, a little exciting, and only half-covered in a Benbow-issue blanket hastily wrapped around her. Through the open door, left, end of the wing, I heard shouting. Over-the-top, raging shouting. She looked small, scared.

So plainly, so plaintively: "Can I come in?"

One second.

"No," I said, and shut the door.

Such things were not to go on at the Benbow. And, largely, didn't. Not visibly. "We are keeping *standards*," Mrs. Patel would say.

Tonight, things felt *different*. Something bordering on happy.

I'd half-laughed, half-cried as I'd cut into the crate MacDonald had shoved into my back seat. Weights. Dumbbells. Collars. Plates—two-and-a-half, five, ten, all the way up to forty-five. MacDonald knew I was an old lifter, gone to seed. And—I hadn't seen it till minutes before on the back seat floor, wrapped in a square cardboard tube, a full-length, full-diameter Olympic bar. Chinese manufacture, a rough edge or two. But a good, solid set. *Enjoy*, MacDonald's card said. *You're on your own for the bench.* I smiled as I read the broken-English instructions for assembly: *Please the slot inserting be.*

I did enjoy. Years, it was, since I'd last hefted any weights. And more since I'd thought of myself as a half-decent amateur. All I did that night was sit upright on my desk chair, push a few five-pounders up and down. Lie on the bed for a dozen ten-pound chest-flys. A few chin-high pull-ups with the Olympic bar. Empty. But I felt that rhythm, that breathing, that rhythm, that breathing…wimpy weight, tonight, and I'd have to keep it wimpy for a while. But *damn*, it felt good.

I was still breathing hard quite a little while after I was done. Letterman was a rerun. As I half-watched, I began thinking about MacDonald's "instructions."

"I hesitate to use the term," he'd said. "I can't *make* you do this."

The deal was: Every night I could, I was to set up shop—binos, scope, night-vision, video, still cameras, folding stool, thermos—at a particular spot inside the railway yards down the south end of the city. The CN yards. And watch. *For* something. But I didn't yet know what the something was, and it didn't seem he was about to tell me yet.

"Canadian National. Thought that would be a nice touch of home for you, Jack," MacDonald said.

For about ten seconds, I thought about summer camping

trips. Kicking Horse campground, just over the Alberta-BC border. Emerald Lake. Takkakkaw Falls, a ribbon of water in a thousand-foot tumble and that glorious spray on the rocks below. The best, for a twelve-year-old heavy-set kid into model trains: the spiral tunnels, where you could see a train boring into the mountain and crossing over itself as it came out. And lying in sleeping bags at night, the four of us, later five and six, the reek of wet canvas, the hiss of rain, and the roar of those five-diesel trains, the howl of those horns, echoing through the night off the walls of Gordon Lightfoot's wild, majestic mountains.

That, of course, was the Canadian Pacific line, the one with all the romance. This was Canadian National, the old, plodding government railway that never got bold till it went private.

Canadian National had bought out the Illinois Central a few years back. Now you could see that curvy CN logo on diesel locomotives, boxcars, container cars, hoppers, car carriers, all the way from Chicago down to New Orleans. Funny to see the word *Canadian* slide along the tracks past towns Mark Twain had painted for Huckleberry Finn. And now, CN was Memphis's third largest employer.

MacDonald had mapped the spot for me.

"How do I get inside the yard?" I asked. "You going to get me some CN company identification and some kind of a guide?"

"Arrangements are being made," he said.

He'd handed me two of those little yellow stickies. On one, he'd written the names of two container companies and about half a dozen multi-digit numbers. On the other, he'd scrawled something that looked a lot like gang graffiti. Only it wasn't for any gang around here. "Where from, then?" I'd asked.

"Elsewhere," he said, and his eyes made clear that was all I was to know.

And then MacDonald told me, his voice conspiratorial: "When you've read these, when you have the numbers memorized, and the little gang symbol thing…"

"What? You gonna get dramatic now?"

"Sorry," he said. "But anyway…eat them."

9.

The lobby. Sunlight through the uncharacteristically open drapes of the east side. Sunlight, in sharp, dust-revealing rays.

I looked for a paper, found yesterday's. It sat beside Mrs. Patel's duct-taped clipboard, so I dared not touch it. Or, for that matter, be caught looking. I heard her in the hall. All I could catch safely was a snippet. Inside: *Wharton promises task force crackdown on human trafficking.*

"LaKenya," Mrs. Patel said, gesturing. "You are washing the windows now, please." She had a way of making the word *please* sound like it wasn't there at all. LaKenya began, not without the occasional barbed look at Mrs. Patel. Bucket. Squeegee. "Too much soap, you are using." Another look, as Mrs. Patel turned elsewhere to address the momentous matter of a dropped towel. I'd never known her first name. Even her badge said: Mrs. Patel.

"Mornin', Mr. Minyard," LaKenya said.

"Morning," I said with a forced cheer. "And it's Jack."

She turned, whispered conspiratorially. "Fresh coffee this morning, Jack," she said. "Saw to it myself."

"Thanks, Kenny," I said. "Pastries, too, I see, for a change." I grabbed and unwrapped a cream cheese danish, took a bite, then remembered—weights, diet, new beginning. I tossed the rest, wrapped in a napkin so Mrs. Patel wouldn't accuse me of waste-fulness. It was pretty good, that bite, notwithstanding it was an undersized, cellophane-imprisoned thing bought, the label said, at Fred's Discount Drugs. Crap food has its virtues. Never spoils. Enough fat and enough sugar can kill anything.

I busied myself fixing my coffee in a styro cup—a big one LaK-enya produced from a cupboard, special for me, to replace the thimble-sized styro sample cups Mrs. Patel favoured. I thanked her. Cream. (Powder. Partially hydrogenated soybean oil. White death.) About eight packets of Splenda. (I'd long since started car-rying my own, and made sure Mrs. P. knew it, thereby enabling me to escape the lecture. "Using two, using two, please. Two, you are allowed.")

As I fumbled to find a stir-stick—management preferred guests use the common spoon, laid in the upturned lid of a mayonnaise jar—Mrs. P. reappeared. "Mr. Jack Minyard," she said—the form she used when, occasionally, she meant to mark respect. "A woman was earlier seeking you."

"A woman?"

Nobody knew where I lived. Even Eileen had only my box number at the Ellendale post office. Far as I knew, anyway. Four years, and no one had *ever* called on me. No one, at least, whom I actually knew, from anywhere.

"Yes. Very nice lady. Very stylish lady."

'Stylish.' I wondered what that meant, in Mrs. P's world. And would that be a *good* thing? It did seem pretty strange, just after seven in the morning.

"Not ten minutes ago. She is asking suite number, I am say-ing we are not revealing suite number, according to policy. She ask if you are in, I am saying I don't know, I think you are not currently on premises. I ask if she is wanting to leave message, parcel, anything. She say no, she is not wishing. But very polite. Very nice, very stylish. Look, now—out veendow."

I turned, caught barely a glimpse. SUV. Moving rightward past the window, rather too fast for a motel parking lot. Looked like an Escalade. Black. No—maybe an extraordinarily dark purple.

Stylish.

10.

19 July, 8:05 a.m.
Starbucks

Bloody insufferable already. The walk from car to door, all by it-self, left me with dark, wet circles under my pits, to match the circles under my eyes.

Left side of the counter, taking all the cushy chairs, what looked to be a pharmaceutical sales team meeting. Easy to spot: impossibly crisp dress shirt, a tall, good-looking salesman type—yeah, there *is* a type—with five or six thirty-something babes, all with product binders, folding portfolios, expensive purses. Heels, lipstick, skirts at just the right length to get them in some busy doctor's office door. And not a glance to me.

Right side: nobody. Not till I saw her in the corner chair. Fragile. Dark hair, which she brushed away from averted eyes. Hand curled around a paper cup. A hesitant hand.

From elsewhere: "Jack."

I had never heard Nikki's voice so small, so near a whisper. But we're all small sometimes. I thought nothing of it. "Yeah, Nick, gimme a venti blonde…" I'd expected some smart-ass re-mark, but it wasn't there.

"'kay."

She slipped behind the capp machine, down to the rack of urns at the far end. I hadn't yet seen her face, but knew some-thing was off.

"On the house, hon," she said when she set the cup down before me. I'd been looking in the direction of the pharmaceutical bunch—a pair of legs, I think. When I turned to face her, Nikki was gone, slipped away in the back.

She was whispering—into a phone, I realized. *What?…Jesus, no. I can't go back there…because I can't…somebody's after me …no, I don't…I don't have the money, I don't have any fucking relatives…I don't want to see anybody…I didn't know who else to call, I…*

I busied myself at the counter. Cinnamon, Splenda, half-and-half. Tossed out the wooden stir stick.

"Jack?" Her voice, still small, came from the back room.

"Yeah!"

"Can I…speak with you?"

"Sure, Nikki."

I stepped up to the counter.

"No. Back here. It's okay, this once." It sounded muffled.

The break room. Half a dozen lockers, aprons, clipboards, schedules. And, at the little table, Nikki sat under a NO SMOKING sign, smoking a cigarette, her hand shaking as she flicked ashes.

She turned toward me. The right side of her face bulbed out, black and purple, her right eye a ring of bruises. The *J* of *Jack* slurred out from her swollen lips.

11.

Nikki had whatever insurance Starbucks grants to those who tough out enough months or years of twenty-five hours a week or less, part-time, and finally bag full-time and benefits. Not the best plan, I was sure, but I was equally sure it beat the crap out of whatever Wal-Mart did. I'd called 'Bucks' district manager, Johnny Broome—a favourite of Lynette's, from some charity board—and he'd sent someone to cover the store. I persuaded him to cut out the whole gotta-fill-out-the-company-form thing, and got her to ER I'd been afraid she's busted her zygomatic arch—the cheekbone that buys those supermodels their supermodel money. I'd seen it happen to a big, dumb Newfie sergeant in Cyprus. It wasn't pretty, and he wasn't right for months. Luckily, the ER doc said, no breaks—just one hell of a bruised mess.

The doc and Nikki both kicked me out of the exam room, so I called MacDonald from the waiting room, left three messages.

At long last, Nikki came out, a nurse on one arm, orderly on the other. Wouldn't get in the wheelchair. "No way," she said. "I'm not some invalid, for—" The look she directed at the orderly said there was no point his insisting any further. Still, she added, "Don't you make me talk."

The pain got to her sharply, suddenly, ripping past whatever the doc had used to dull it. A nurse handed me two prescriptions and some kind of high-end, fancy icebag contraption that would hit her insurance at fifteen times the drugstore price. The doc gave me a shrug and said he was handing off to Nikki's doubtless nonexistent primary care physician.

A stop at the pharmacy, then I asked her, "Where's home?" I hadn't thought till that moment about where she lived.

A deep wince, silent tears, and a hoarse "your place" was all I got.

I did ask questions.

Who? Nothing.

What with? Nothing from Nikki. But the nurse had told me she'd said something about a two-by-four the guy had picked up by the BFI bin back of 'Bucks.

Why? Any idea? The slightest shake of her head, and another wince.

Why the hell did you keep working? I asked her, and got "It's what I do."

Then: Who were you talking to on the phone in the break room?

Her face said: Don't you know?

Dumbly, I didn't.

I knew better than to protest the destination. Safe enough—my room held two queen beds. I laid her out in the spare, gave her three of the pills she was only to have one of, and that was that.

Save for the little kiss on her forehead and the pained little smile that came in its wake.

12.

19 July, 10:08 p.m.
Raines Road, South Memphis

Saskatoon, on a hot day, cools at night. Memphis, on a hot day, doesn't. And South Memphis, somehow, stays even hotter. Sometimes, during the night, you can hear gunfire.

The neon sign out on Raines said grocery. No name. The neon sign by the door said open, but the look of the place said closed. Till the kid, eleven or twelve, came out, hopped on his banana-seat bike and pedaled across the gravel lot into the dark with what looked like a clutch of red licorice sticks in his shirt pocket and a brown bag with a couple of quart Colt 45s. You'd see these little groceries everywhere in South Memphis, even where the regular streets gave way to long stretches of what looked like countryside, hiding shotgun houses here and there amid the brush. Rattletrap little oases, if you will. Beer. Cigarettes. Lottery. Food stamps...ok.

A stunned streetlamp hung high, alone, on a telephone pole. In the trees looming about, insects scratched, hummed, sang, in bass, tenor, soprano, the higher voices at random, the lower in layers of rhythm, rise and fall, counting the seconds and counting, I suspected, the age of the earth. We humans, here, I'd come to realize since embracing the South, were merely tenants. I was standing here alone, listening to the landlords. Across the broken concrete where I'd parked, hundreds, thousands of small, identical beetles—it was that time of year again—hastened on errands too urgent for them to give me any notice. I crushed no small number of them underfoot, but it made no difference. A light in the store's barred window flashed. Miller time.

Oddly, given the heat, I shivered.

Cars came. Cars went. Car doors slammed. Pairs of men, often as not. Some laughing. Some silent. Some who looked my way. One who started to walk over. Then thought better of it.

Then MacDonald.

"Could we not meet in a more respectable place, Mac? The Starbucks at Winchester and Hack's Cross is open till eleven, you know."

"This on the low-down, brother." He sounded more hood than Germantown, tonight. He'd been to see *her*. Oh, hell, I wasn't even supposed to know.

MacDonald walked over. "Gimme one a those." He didn't even smoke. Not really. But I'd seen this before. It usually *meant* something. I held out the pack, BiC. He did the dew. Coughed.

"Smoke up now," he said. "I don't want you smokin' on the job."

"Oh, the railroad yard is no-smoking?" I said dumbly.

"I don't know," he said.

"Got my ID?"

"I got everything you need."

I gave him *that* look.

"Got your shit together, Jack?"

"You mean my binocular shit, my night-vision shit, my middle-of-the-night lunch-in-a-bag shit?" I asked.

"All that shit," he said.

"So you gonna take me to the gate, give me the ID, introduce me to whomever will be—"

"Something like that." Which, in MacDonald-speak, means: Nothing like that.

I was to leave Mitzi at the grocery, though MacDonald had me pull her around back, by the open rear door. "I know the guy," he said. "Owes me a favour. Your car be all right."

My stuff loaded into Mac's car, we drove past what I'd always thought was the main south entrance to the CN yards.

"Uh, Mac—"

"Yours not to reason why, brother."

Brother, I knew, meant I was getting in deeper.

MacDonald pulled in to an anonymous, recessed gateway in the chain-link fence surrounding the yard. A forested stretch of Raines. Got out, reached in the back seat for a massive pair of bolt-cutters, at which point the last drop of illusory legitimacy in all of this drained away.

"I suppose I'd best not ask," I said as Mac got back in, pulled the car through the gate and a couple of car-lengths along the wooded road.

"Best not," he said, walked back, drew the wings of the gate shut, and returned. The car rocked in the ruts, splashed through a couple of pools of water, the car frame creaking as the road roughened. Presently, as the woods began to open, he killed the lights, but still crept forward, just into the open area, parked behind a weedy pile of sand awaiting resumption of some forgotten construction project.

MacDonald looked around nervously as I gathered my stuff, now mostly shoved into a big daypack. "Ready?" he asked.

"Not at all," I said.

"Good," he said.

He walked me about fifty yards ahead, a narrow sand-and-gravel walk alongside a deep ditch emitting a rather rancid aroma. What little we said was whispered. We stopped beside an old barrel, a couple of staves missing.

"Another fifty yards," he said, pointing. "You'll see a second barrel, like this one, only tumped over. That's where you'll cross the ditch and go inside the fence. You'll see a dirt pile and a big bush beside. You can set up there."

"And how do I get across this ditch? Can't really tell, but that water looks deep." I said.

"You're always telling me you're 'infantry," he said. "Death-dealing son of a gun. First in the field, second to none, up the Guards, all that."

"Yeah, but I'm *old* infantry."

"Always thinking of you first, Jack. I done built you a little bridge myself, yesterday. Big old wide plank. Sturdy, too. You can't miss it."

"Don't suppose you made me a gate in the fence on the other side."

"Time, as it happens, Jack, did not permit. But, then, I know how much you enjoy the whole do-it-yourself thing." I hadn't even seen him carrying the bolt cutters till he handed them to me.

"Lucking fluvvly," I said. "Break-and-enter."

"I envy your ever-increasing repertoire of occupational skills," MacDonald said. "Speaking of which…"

"What?"

"You're not carrying your piece, are you?"

"Course I am."

Even in the dark, I could see him hold out his hand. I pulled the clip-holster off my belt, handed it over.

"Geez, MacDonald."

"Break and enter *with* a weapon?" he said. "That'd be like…"

"Burglary," I filled in. "Can I keep my folding knife?"

"If you promise to think of it as a letter opener."

"Remind me why I'm doing this?" I asked.

"Uh…truth, justice, and the American way?" MacDonald said.

"I'm not even an American, remember? What else?"

"Chinese buffets," he said. "Saville Row shirts. Dates with fabulous babes."

There was nothing I could say.

Except: "When will you be back to pick me up?"

MacDonald shrugged. "When I'm done."

Her, again. The bugger was going *back*. I'd be out here, and he'd be—

Now there was absolutely nothing to say.

I found the barrel, the plank-bridge. Got across without so much as a dampened boot. As luck would have it, a slice of fence was actually down, and I could step across. I stashed the bolt cutters back on the safe side of the ditch, under a piece of ancient scrap plywood, crossed back to the trouble side, set up my folding stool, and settled in for the night.

I knew what I was watching for. Watched. Yawned. Watched. And didn't see a damn thing.

MacDonald came at dawn, as I sprang from half-awake to full, courtesy of some howling cur, somewhere behind, quite a way off.

I was dog-tired, soaked in sweat, my socks were soggy inside my old combat boots. I'd spent the night vaguely unnerved by things moving in the brush behind me, sometimes right past me in the grass and gravel beside the dirt pile. Armadillos, I suspected. *Not* cute. And the damn things carry leprosy. I felt scratchy and filthy, and wanted nothing more than a shower and bed. Best I'd get, though, was a shower and a trip out to the Bartlett stretch of Summer to see Eileen—she'd texted me to come in, early as I could. Not asked, mind you. A summons. There was a difference. Ask…you could wander in whenever. Summons…be there, bells on, oh-dark-thirty.

I mumbled some crap as I walked across the downed fence and the ditch toward MacDonald, the straps of my daypack dragging on the ground.

Then I saw it. Rooftop, gleaming in the morning sun. An old, ramshackle two-storey house on a rise behind the trees, maybe a quarter mile distant from the containers I'd been watching all night, watching them stacked, unstacked, restacked at the hands of the two huge moving dolly cranes, most of the containers left standing, still, waiting all night, as I had, for Lord knows what.

The house, once yellow, but mostly peeled, looked like it was still occupied. The light in the upstairs window said so, as did the car parked between the house and the swing-less, rusty swing set.

MacDonald saw me look at the house, looked away, said nothing. His silence said: *Something*.

He heard my unspoken question.

"We'll talk," he said.

"When?" I asked, and he answered, "I don't know."

On the way out of the place, through the gate, all the way to the grocery store a mile or more down Raines, not one word. Not even about Nikki.

13.

21 July, 9:06 a.m.
The Inn — Out of Sorts — Eileen's

I'd stolen an hour of sleep anyway, Eileen's summons notwith-standing. Bowl of Cheerios. What the hell, I'm late as it is—set up the laptop on the desk.

Nikki snored, moaned a little.

Checked my email—first time in two days. Meet horny housewives in your neighbourhood. You, too, can make fifteen thousand a month, doing *absolutely nothing*. Enlarge this body part, shrink that. Click—junk. Most of the other traffic was from a single address. Sweet emails. May-the-Lord-bless-you emails. Hope-you-don't-mind emails. Old-time's-sake emails. So-sorry-to-hear emails. Hope-you-are-well emails. Would-love-for-us-to-get-together emails. Wanted-to-bring-you-a-casserole emails. Damn—I'd get to the bottom of this.

Kill two birds with one stone. *This* nonsense first. Then what-ever it was Eileen wanted to see me about. So I hit SEND on a vague reply, then drove over to Red Line.

I opened the front door oh-so gingerly, so Eileen's cute little jingle bells didn't ring. Shushed Jackie before she could say a word, and barged on back, plopped myself in a chair, facing Eileen.

She didn't look up. "Practising our stealth skills, are we?"

"Did some of that last night," I said. "Feeling kinda done with all that, for today. What are you practising?"

She looked up. Her face asked. Then answered her own question. "She's contacted you?"

"Numerous times," I said.

Eileen feigned a smile. "Good, good. So you two will be getting together, then?"

"I've no doubt."

"Good. Well. Reason I called you in—"

"We're not done with this yet, Eileen."

"Oh?"

"Question, Eileen. Barbara Jean McCorkle—does she drive a Cadillac?"

"No. Um, more like an SUV, I think. An…*Escapade*?"

Come off it, honey. Ex-cop. She knew her cars better than that.

"Escalade," I said. "Black?"

"Um…not quite. More like a—"

"Really, really dark purple."

"*Could* be…yes. I think that's it."

"This is bullshit, Eileen."

"I don't appreciate that kind of lang—"

"And I don't appreciate games."

"Then maybe you won't appreciate this, either."

She handed me a larger-than-usual envelope, flap open. Cheque. Twelve hundred dollars and change, for the divorce case. Two months at the Benbow. Or a month plus eats and gas, maybe even a few revenue stamps for my collection. She passed it along with a card, in a pretty, perfect hand, turquoise fountain pen. Simple. *Thank you, Jack, for a wonderful job. Please know we love you…Eileen.*

I didn't know anyone loved me.

Deep breath. "I'm sorry, Eileen. I owe you better. I'm just…"

"Tired," she filled in.

"Not an excuse," I said.

"No," she said. "But perhaps a cause. She's been pestering you with calls?"

"No," I told her. "Just emails."

"Well, good. Because I didn't give her your phone number, Jack."

"Thank you."

"Not yet, anyway."

"And what would prompt you to give her my number?"

"Your consent."

"Why would I give that?"

"Because I'm asking."

"Asking because…"

"Because she…needs…and because, well…*you* need."

"You don't mean…"

She looked at me querulously, then the realization broke across her face. "That I'm playing matchmaker? No. Definitely. No. Good God, no. Didn't even think of that angle. Didn't think you'd think…*I'm* sorry, Jack."

"No sorries required, Eileen. If what you say is true. And if Barbara Jean McCorkle has the same understanding."

"She's happily…she's married, Jack."

"Still married to…"

"Um…far as I know, Jack." She knew, all right.

"So what does she want, Eileen?"

"You know Barbara Jean," Eileen said. "She's not happy unless she's helping."

"'Helping.' Like the Boy Scout who helped the little old lady across the street—"

"—even though she didn't want to go." Eileen laughed. "That

THORAZINE BEACH » **71**

is true. The thing of it is, I guess, is that she's not happy unless she's *involved*."

"Involved in what?"

"Well, in…giving to people. Doing things for people. *You* know…"

"Back to the question. What does she want?"

"Well, I think she really does want to…to see you…to help you if she can…to…"

"Bring me a casserole?"

Eileen laughed again. "If she gives you a choice, go for the green bean with the almonds and the crunchy cracker crust. It's pretty good. It's a hit around our house…my house." Her smile faded, took a few seconds to come back.

"I'll remember that," I answered.

"Of course, the thing about casseroles…" she said.

"Is what?"

"Well, you've got to wash the dish. Then you've got to give it back."

"Barbara Jean McCorkle and I are not *just* going to slurp a thirty-minute Americano at Starbucks, are we?"

"Umm…I expect not."

"There's going to be a whole…*thing* here, isn't there?"

We both started to laugh. "Yeah," she said. "I reckon there is."

I made my smile go away. "One more time, back to the question. What…" Big, dramatic pause. "does she want?"

"Bring you a little cheer. A casserole, maybe?"

"That's *to* me, Eileen. What does she want…" I love pauses. "*from* me?"

There's a certain look crosses Eileen's face when she's about to say something glib or smartass. Whatever it was Les had fallen in love with, it surely included that. "*Other* than her casserole dish back," I said.

"Just some information, Jack. Just that. I think."

"And whatever that…*information* is, Eileen, I presume it's not the sort can be gathered from a desk and a phone and a high-speed internet connection."

"No."

"How much do you know?" I asked.

"Truly, Jack, next to nothing. I asked, but you know Barbara Jean—she did all the talking."

I nodded. "Way less informative than it was long."

"She came in at four that day," Eileen said. "And we weren't out till seven."

"And she said…?"

"Like I say, next to nothing. There was something she wanted you to 'look into.'" A big pair of air-quotes. "Said she wanted a real…"

"Real what?"

Her mouth made a tiny smile. "'Gumshoe,' is what she said, Jack."

"That the actual word?" I felt my eyes roll.

"As God is my witness, Jack."

"Those only exist in fiction," I said. "As well you know."

"Not in *her* mind."

"I need a trench coat for this?"

"And a fedora hat as well, I expect, Jack."

"Jesus."

"You might need him, too." Her face was dead serious.

"What do you mean by that?"

"I don't," Eileen replied, "*mean*…anything. I just have this… feeling."

So did I.

14.

21 July, 11:30 a.m.
A Cozy Wee Place for Two

I stopped for ice cream on the way back to the Benbow. Breyers. Vanilla bean. "Got to be the vanilla bean," Nikki had once told me. "No bean, it's just, well... vanilla." That and chocolate sauce. That'd perk the girl up, I thought. I'd noticed that morning the swelling had already gone down considerably. Her face was still, half of it anyway, one giant bruise, and it had worn pain, even in her sleep.

I unlocked the door as quietly as I could, thinking she might still be sleeping. I felt for the overhead light switch, thought better of it, turned on the little desk lamp I'd bought.

No Nikki. Just a note. *Thank you, Jack, for everything. Just a little cozy in here, is all. Don't worry—I've got somebody...Love, Nikki.*

"Somebody." I had my own idea who.

I thought about tucking the ice cream—a gallon's worth—in the fridge. Then I thought better of that, too, hoofed it over to the office, found LaKenya, plucked a smile from somewhere, and passed it off as a gift I'd dreamed up just for her.

My consolation: ramen noodles in the microwave.

15.

23 July, 2:00 p.m.
Nikki, Don't Lose That Number

"Jack." It sounded like: *Hey, you*.

"Nikki?"

"Yeah. Listen, Jack—"

"How'd you get my number?"

"Phht," she said. "I've had it for years." Swelling must be down, I thought—the muffle was gone from her voice.

"You never gave me yours."

"Oh, I'd never give *that* out. Not to just anyone."

Sigh. "So…"

"Anyway, she's here."

"Where?"

"At the counter, idiot."

"Who?"

"*You* know."

"No. Who?"

"Too classy for you, buster."

Some kind of titter in the background.

"Name?" I asked.

"Some uppity Collierville chick. Kind of a babe."

"This uppity Collierville chick have a handle?"

"Some triple-barreled, three-ring circus kind of a thing. Southern as pecan pie."

"Wouldn't be Barbara Jean McCorkle, by any chance?"

"Bingo."

"She want to talk to me?"

"No, Jack. She drove all the way in from Hooterville for burnt coffee and stale cheesecake."

"Well, put her on, then, please."

"Hell, no. I'm not burning my cell minutes on *you*, bozo. Thing is, Babs, here, wants to *see* you—not listen to your dulcet tones through the crackle of AT&T."

"Was she *expecting* me?"

"She is now."

"Well, she didn't have an appointment."

"She got one now."

"How?"

"Told her I'd make one."

"What are you—my private secretary?"

"You wish. But I'm not wearing that French maid's outfit."

"What a relief," I said. "The butler will appreciate that. When's the appointment?"

"Now, fool. You're late. Get your ass in here."

Click.

My ass got.

Barbara Jean McCorkle, all five-ten of her, rose to greet me. Six-two or three, if you counted the heels. And they did get my attention— she'd been a flat-soled, long-sleeved, buttoned-to-the-neck church lady, last I'd seen her. I knew she was just shy of me, in age, and you have to be something to carry off a leather mini if you're that vintage. And she was *something*, I had to admit. Different look, for sure. Fine vintage.

She'd saved the two soft seats in the corner, and motioned me into one as she sat in the other, a little round table between us. Her blouse gapped, and I started thinking: boob job.

"So…" She leaned in. "Jack." She smiled. "Lovely to see you." She did something throaty and wonderful and nineteen-thirties with the 'o' in *lovely*.

"You too," I said lamely, sure I couldn't invest my own *lovely* with what she'd given hers.

"Um…your voice is different, Barbara Jean."

Smile. "Speech. Elocutions lessons," she said with obnoxiously immaculate articulation. *Private* lessons, she told me, with more than a touch of pride on private. A Miss Mary Hailsham, she told me. Old school. "England, you know," she said in a want-to-be-British way.

Nikki wanted *in* on this, it was apparent. Last time she'd indulged anyone with table service was Mac's cup of tea a few days back. And before that, months ago, a guy in a wheelchair—and even he got a sigh and a roll of Nikki's eyes. Quite the conversation they'd had, Nikki and Barbara Jean, apparently. "Another latte for you, BJ," Nikki said, setting it down. "On the house. And you, Jack? My treat."

"Oh, my," I said. "Your discretion, Nikki. Thank you."

Nikki banged off something resembling a curtsy—for my benefit, I recognized, a kind of pantomimed sarcasm.

"'Bee-Jay,'" Barbara quoted. "Charming, isn't she? I haven't been called that in years. Never used to like that, till now—it always felt so…"

"Unseemly?" I filled in.

"Yes, I suppose so," she said.

Was that a faint blush on those cheeks?

"But I like it from *her*," she said.

I smiled blankly.

"Lovely girl."

I held that smile.

"I love young ladies like that," she said. "It's the spunk, I think. Have you known her long, Jack?"

"Been spunked for several years, now. Since about the time—"

"Oh, yes, since…well," she said in a let's-not-talk-about-it way.

"Right."

"So…"

"Yes."

"Jack, it's been a very—"

"Long time, indeed," I said, nodding. I wanted to ask something in the what-the-hell's-the-point-of-*this* vein, but nothing I was composing in my head matched the woman before me, even less the one I'd remembered. I've got rude, somehow, in my old age.

"Well, Jack, I suppose you've been wondering why…"

Thank you, Jesus. "I had been."

"Well," she said. "I did want to say hello, did want to bring you a casserole"—she laughed at that, turned serious. "And talk to you about…something."

Portentous. High control needs, my old shrink would have said. It was meant to make me ask. "And what is that something, Barbara Jean? Exactly."

"Blackmail," she said with surprising directness, looked me square in the eye.

I looked back, eye to eye. "Details?" I said.

"That's the gumshoe in you," she said, smiling again. "I'd have thought you'd say, 'Oh, Barbara Jean, I'm *so* sorry'—something like that."

There she was, the Barbara Jean of old—always needing to correct you on *something*.

"I do, of course, feel that way. Must be a terrible—"

"It is!"

I leaned in, the way she had, nodding to Nikki's bringing my coffee. A tall Americano, I noted, recalling that 'tall,' in Buck-Speak, means 'short'. Uselessly small, criminally unflavourful. No cream, no sugar, and not a thing I'd ever drink voluntarily. Nikki avoided my look.

"Barbara Jean, you're clearly here to ask my help, my advice, something. In order to help, it's details I need. Not meaning to be rude or presumptuous, but that's where we need to go."

"Shall I begin at the beginning?" She looked like she was about to start back in high school.

"Start in the middle," I said. Then, remembering Eileen's description of their talk, I decided I'd better manage this more closely. "What—exactly—are they blackmailing you *for*? Paint me a real tight picture."

My control-tactic registered on her face unpleasantly. "All right," she said, a little coldness creeping in. "You want pictures…" She reached into a slim leather case set on the floor, pulled out a file folder. "Here." She slapped them down on table. "You'll want to make sure we're not seen or heard," she said.

I looked. Listened. No one else inside the place but Nikki. I asked her to switch the PA to jazz and turn it up some.

Opened the folder. First picture: The girl couldn't have been more than eleven, even allowing for the smaller sizes you see in Latinas. Couldn't tell whether she was pretty or not, in any sense a guy like me could relate to. First, I'm attracted to women, not girls, usually somewhere between the wrong side of forty and Barbara Jean's age. Second: This poor wee thing was painted up like an aging transvestite in an Amsterdam red-light window.

I looked at Barbara Jean, trying to appear expressionless. "Go on," she said, motioning.

Two: Thai, Malaysian, something. Seventeen, maybe. Poured

into a blue lycra tube dress with a red-lips kisses motif, and—I didn't *get* this part—clutching what looked like a toilet brush. Bad lighting. Amateur shot. And a facial expression that rolled resentment and embarrassment and perplexity all into one.

Three: Filipina, looked like. Mid-teens. Pretty, this one—but in a sweet, baby-sister kind of way. She was squeezed into something that looked like a prom dress for the gal voted Most Likely to Be Busted for Soliciting. She looked, nonetheless, still innocent. Smiling, wide-eyed. As if all she knew were that the dress was the prettiest thing she'd seen in her life, she was grateful to be given it, and she felt like *somebody* wearing it.

Eighteen, twenty pictures in all. Every one an eight-by-ten glossy. Interestingly, some colour, some black and white. Some digital, and some, it was clear, good old fashioned film enlargements. Every one a girl or young woman—almost all something other than Caucasian—dressed to, as it were, impress. Impress in one particular way, to one very particular kind of audience.

You be nice to the gentlemen, Fancy…and they'll be nice to you.

"You've called the police, of course."

"Oh. No. Certainly not," she said in the most matter-of-fact tone. "You see, they're in on it."

One last picture. A guy. Balding. Middle-aged and a bit beyond. An odd cross between a man with money, confidence, and the kind of guy who sells aluminum siding. I looked at her.

"My husband," she said. "Clayton." A faint smile that came a little late.

I smiled back, equally faint, hoping my smile didn't convey what had just occurred to me: He was the guy I'd seen with His Eminence, at the New Nam King.

"So…blackmail," I said.

She nodded.

"Blackmail of…?"

"I'm…not sure."

"Blackmail *for*…?"

"Well, money, of course," she said in a silly-question way.

"How much?"

"They haven't asked."

"Who's 'they,' Barbara Jean?"

"They…haven't said."

"No calls, no note?"

"Um…not…not as yet."

"And I am investigating…*what*? Exactly."

"It's a bit…" I was beginning to hate the way she paused as if searching for words, and the way I'd caught myself doing it, too. "Delicate," she said.

"Always is. So…"

She hesitated.

"Look," I said, sharply enough to regret it. I re-set my tone. "What I mean, Barbara Jean, is, I need to know where I'm looking, who I'm looking at, and what I'm looking for."

She nodded, gathered herself. "The where is determined by the whom, and the whom is…"

I ventured a little, to fill it in. "Clayton," I said.

She looked back at me, expressionless, and I knew I was right. "And what am I looking at the whom *for*?"

Kleenex. Face turned away. Incipient tear. I half-thought it was contrived. But only half. "I think he may be, how can I put this…implicated…in something."

Christ, we're all *implicated*. I breathed. "Barbara Jean," I said. "I need to know whatever it is you know, if I'm going to do anything."

She sighed. "There's been a good deal of money about the house, lately."

"What does your husband do?"

"He's in real estate development," she said. "Federman Properties. He owns it now." I knew the company. A few strip mall units—you'd see their signs here and there. Some properties they owned, some they just brokered. Big enough business for a guy to make a hell of a good living. But not *Lifestyles of the Rich and Famous*.

"And what—I presume there's *something* you haven't told me yet—is this thing he's 'implicated' in."

"As I said, Jack, there's been a good deal of money about the house."

"By which you mean…"

"Cash," she said behind a sip from her cup.

"And by 'cash' you mean…?"

Straight out, without a blink: "Briefcases full."

"Hmm," I said. "Like, enough to get you to Barbados and back?"

"Enough to get you to the moon and back."

"Does he know you know?"

She shrugged. "Things haven't been…" A bit of the old Barbara Jean came back, the Southern woman ever in search of a discreet way to put things. "There are inevitable strains in a marriage." A deliberated pause. "You understand, Jack, I think, hmm?"

Jab. "Yeah, I do."

"I'm sorry, Jack. Forgive me, but…whatever did happen between you and…Lynette?"

I wasn't willing to play. "Inevitable strains," I said. "Now, the million-dollar question. What's with the girls?"

"Clayton started a second business," she said.

"Import-export?"

Her face said she didn't appreciate the sarcastic edge. "It was nannies at first," she said. "Au pair girls, that sort of thing."

"At first…" I prodded.

"Then I began to suspect…well, you've seen the pictures."

"Yes. And where did you see them?"

"In one of the…briefcases."

"You mean, actual *briefcases* full of…?"

"Yes," she said, and looked right at me. "Clayton has a built-in gun cabinet—I don't even know the combination. He likes target shooting, hunting, that sort of—"

"Thing, yes. And—"

"And one day he'd left…well, it was open, and—"

"You looked."

"It was wide open, and there was one of the guns missing and, well, I thought it was so odd to find a briefcase in…so naturally I…I looked."

"You didn't ask him?"

"Well, as I said, there's a certain…*stress*…in *any* marriage."

"And a little more now," I said.

More Kleenex. "I love my husband," she said. "Notwithstanding…"

"Of course," I said. It sounded like token sympathy, even to me. "And you want…"

"I want to know," she said, plucking up some nerve and quickly losing it. "And I want this to be over."

Barbara Jean gathered the pics, returned them to the folder, the folder to her case. "You are," she said, "trustworthy, are you not?"

She wanted an answer. I didn't give it.

"Mr. Minyard," she said—where did *that* come from? "I've come to expect a certain degree of loyalty…" I closed my eyes. The words sounded like Isaac Breitzen in lipstick.

She looked at me. I looked back, not quite knowing what my face said.

Her face relaxed—a bit deliberately, I thought—then took on a touch of Southern coquette. "I'm sorry, Jack, it's all so…" She looked away. Lip. Eyes down. Kleenex yet again.

I admit: I'm a sucker for certain things, certain images. Mike Hammer, Spenser—*they* can be tough, bar-bourbon, unfiltered. Me, as a detective—I'm totally decaf and whipped cream. I leaned in and touched her arm. "No. Barbara Jean…*I'm* sorry."

"Let's go outside a minute," she said. We did, sat at one of the tables under a green umbrella that cast no meaningful shade, and if anything added to the heat. I'd never seen Barbara Jean smoke. But she pulled out a package of Nat Sherman's—black, gold-tipped, expensive as all get-out. She offered me one but I stuck with my own. Her lighter, I saw, was a Dunhill, antique, gold. I flicked my own yellow BiC. The way she let me was, in its way, revealing. As if she'd *learned* it, learned it in some kind of calculated, dress-for-success way, from the kind of women who know how to impress men in cocktail lounges. *Touch the man's hand lightly as he lights it…that's it…just a gentle brush.* That, and a warm, smoky smile. "I'm a late starter," she said. "But I've learned, it calms me. And I do like…" She smiled again. "…a certain style."

Two grand in cash and an hour later—yes, I did wonder where the cash came from, but I didn't ask—I'd agreed to a bunch of stuff I shouldn't have. *Strict* confidentiality. *No* police. *Daily* reports—in person, never by phone. I was to keep working whatever jobs Eileen gave me—and I tucked MacDonald in there, too, though we never mentioned him. That, she said, would be part of the cover. *No one*, she said, could know I was working for her. In return for this: two grand a week, just like today, till I was done.

"Well, Jack," she said. "I am *so* grateful. And—look at the time …you'll want to be getting started, I expect."

Nikki came out the door, a melmac plate in her left hand, spoon in her right, mouth full, plopped herself down at our table. "Hell of a casserole, BJ," she said, and turned to me. "Jack, I'll give you the dish out of the fridge, coupla days, when I'm done and run it through the diswasher, and you can take it back to BJ."

16.

22, 23, 24, 25, 26, 27, 28, 29, 31 July Night Out Back in the Yard, Birdwatching

"Come on, MacDonald. It rained all last night. Third night in a row it's—"

"Jack I need you to…"

I need I need I need.

"You are cashing stamps like crazy, here, MacDonald."

"I know, I know, I know."

We'd both cashed a hundred, a thousand, between the two of us, all those years. And had still more to go, I hoped. Bitching was just part of the deal.

"I saved your ass, MacDonald."

"I saved *your* ass, Chubby Checker."

True, both counts, and more than once. Without all that saving, there'd be two less asses in town, no doubt.

I'd stopped asking why and what for. The best I'd squeezed out of MacDonald was some cockamamie thing about him working with the feds on "one of those importing-pelts, illegal-poaching, take-no-whales, save-the-tiger things. *You* know, Jack—you go for that shit, you get the Greenpeace calendar."

He'd been speaking for a few months, now, in terms like *commission*, *task force*. It was mostly here-and-there stuff. Mentions, allusions. It was all fuzzy—annoyingly vague, at times. Crap. I'd begun to wonder which it really was—whether he wanted to tell me, not tell me, or half-tell me. I'd settled on the last, and tried not to prod or poke. I'd filed a few snippets away. *Wildlife*, he'd said a couple of times. Even, once, the World Wildlife Federation. Then: *Smuggling.*

His story was a steaming pile of Bravo Sierra—a lot of it, anyway. That much I knew. But the one part I bought, straight-up, was what I got when I asked him why *he* wasn't the one out here suffering. All that patent-leather MacDonald bravado drained from his face. "All I can tell you is, there's something dirty, Jack. Inside. *Very* dirty. Very…*threatening*. I think they're…watching me." That pulled me halfway in. Then that one word, his word, *scared*, made up the rest. Tough bastard. Patrol car. Burglary. Narcotics. Vice. Homicide, even, for a little stretch. I'd *never* heard him say that word. *Scared*. What could I do?

And so it came to pass. One more night. Half-hot air, cold rain, rattling on my old Canadian Forces poncho. Days before, I'd rigged a little lean-to, one I could set up and take down each night, tucked in between the big dirt pile and a bush. A little brush for cammo, break up the shape. Each morning I'd hide my lean-to, poncho and poles and a couple of lengths of rope, under the edge of a stack of debris, dig it out again at night. Rain pants, rain jacket, some cammo paint and cut-up pieces of ghillie suit to mask the shape and shine and silhouette of my gear. All of it surplus-store crap—yet another benefit to life on Summer Avenue.

After the third night, I'd stopped relying on MacDonald to bring me, park me, pick me up, and had begun parking my car at an all-night Mapco I'd found three blocks along Raines, the other direction from the grocery. I gave the night guy ten each time to watch my car. Sweet deal, he thought. And I could use the exercise. I made up a story about going out for hours-long walks, about nighttime bird-watching. Silly, that—I needn't have given him that, he likely didn't give a rodent's rear. But the story did explain all the gear I was lugging. I even tucked a birding book under my arm the first night, and passionately outlined my intense desire to photograph the secret mating rituals of the yellow-breasted corncrake. The guy bought the ten, if not the tale. And MacDonald appreciated, he said, my self-sufficiency. Which meant, I suppose, he appreciated the extra chances to be with *her*.

My instructions from Mac were: Look for a full-size container from either of two specific container companies—Hanjin, and Hapag-Lloyd. Both common, though Lloyd a little the less so. Look for serial numbers that ended in certain three-digit strings: 481, 603, 709—there were a few others, long since committed to memory. Look for one of these containers that the crane plops in *this exact* position. Mac had drawn me a diagram: the position I'd be looking for was to be lined up under the left edge of the main container-yard building and, beyond that, the tallest radio mast on top of the hump yard control tower. Then, look for the gang graffiti. *Specific* gang graffiti, spray-painted right under or right beside the container company's name. Then: two more things. One, look for a fifty-three-foot trailer, a Crete, way on the left, darker end of the trailer lot, near the south gate, where they hardly ever parked anything. Two, if I saw the Crete there, call MacDonald. Stat.

Funny symbol, that gang thing. Didn't look like any Memphis gang's, or any gang I knew of, but then MacDonald or any cop would tell you there's a new gang a week in town. This one MacDonald had once called "Three-six-gamma," the shape he'd drawn on the yellow stickie no one was ever to see:

Circles and crosses appear all the time in gang graffiti. I'd sat through MacDonald's own seminar on the subject, a couple of years back. The symbols were mostly more complicated than this one. You'd get a circle cut up by an X, numbers would mean addresses, dates, times of gang meetings, and whichever quadrant the number was in would tell you which—address, date, or time.

When he'd first shown me, I'd been suspicious about the gamma-thing. "Gangs do Greek letters?"

"Has been known," he said. "But not generally, no. They're not desperately literate. Not so much interested in your classical languages and lit."

"Not a Memphis-based gang, Mac. Is it?"

"Umm...no. Least...I don't think so."

"Where from, then?"

"Uh, Seattle, we think."

We, indeed. I'd already made a bet with myself that, if I were to call the Seattle gangs unit—Tacoma, Vancouver, anywhere up that way—they'd tell me they'd never heard of anything called three-six-gamma. I could have called, could have faxed, would have got *some* kind of an answer, even without being a cop. But if I got that answer, I'd know MacDonald was lying. I was willing to know that. But not to *know* it. Not beyond a reasonable doubt. Not beyond that point where every guy in the firing squad gets to believe *he's* the one who got the blank round.

Sat. Watched. Coffee from my thermos. Sat. Tuna sandwich. Sat. Watched. Yawned. Snickers bar, nice and hard, from my mini-cooler. I stopped after one bite, tossed the rest into the outer dark. Contraband.

More than one night I'd seen Hanjins and Lloyds bearing numbers with what seemed the right three final digits. But an eight, more closely inspected, became a three—that sort of thing. Once, I'd seen what I thought was the symbol, but the wrong serial, the wrong company's container. False alarms both, MacDonald told me. Don't worry about it. How the hell could he be *that* sure?

Sometime after midnight, 31st July to the 1st of August. The rain let up a little.

Sounds. Not unusual. Cracking branch. Movement, small animal—there was *something* here, I'd learned, that was attracting feral cats. Quiet again. Right now, no movement over in the yard. The craneman's coffee break, I assumed. The hiss of the drizzling rain. The layer of steam it made over the ground.

My head jerked. I heard what I hoped had been only a few seconds of snoring. The cranes were moving again. My videocam's tripod had tipped over, the camera doing a close-up digital documentary of my dirt pile.

Sounds. Behind. Unusual. Foot on gravel—definitely not animal. Other foot on gravel—heavier. Coming nearer, but other side of the pile, other side of the ditch. Stopped. Froze. Footfall again. Light. Heavier. And, in between, the gentlest little thud. Slow. Light. Little thud. Heavier.

Waiting.

"Don't you fucking move."

Loud enough, directed enough I knew he meant me, knew exactly where I was. Railway cop? No, no—that little thump, it sounded for all the world like a cane, of all the bloody things.

Then: Unmistakable. Chuck-chick. Pump-action shotgun.

"I'm coming over," the voice said, some gravel in it. And more than a hint of an experience I surely didn't want to be on the wrong end of.

I knew for sure when he started onto the board-bridge Mac had laid for me. Light. Cane. Heavy. Not a railway cop. Not a Memphis cop. Not anyone with a badge. Not a nice grown-up you can run to.

"Don't you fucking move."

I breathed.

I moved.

I ran, as much as a man of sixty with eighty-five extra pounds can be said to *run* at all. Busted out of my lean-to, left all my gear. My toes tripped on rocks, branches, gopher holes. More than once I fell, my hands, arms, scraped each time. More than once, I banged my shins on what I guessed was scrap steel, broken concrete. A rip on a protruding piece of rebar.

Diabetes. Peripheral neuropathy. You have no idea. The skin on my shins screamed.

"God damn you!" behind me. And I wondered whether he mightn't get that wish. *Jesus Jesus Jesus*, I said, whether aloud or inside I didn't know, and couldn't tell whether it was swearing or prayer.

The flash, first. Then the sound of the blast. Cocked. Flash. Blast. Shot at twice, now.

I took breathless cover behind a mound of dirt. *He'd* had the advantage, still had it. I'd been silhouetted the whole way against the blazing lights of the container yard, and would be again whenever I got up. I stayed low, looked *around* the mound, rather than over. I felt inside my lower pant leg for what was running there, felt it on my fingers. I couldn't see, so I tasted. Blood, all right. But not enough that he'd hit me—just a bad bump.

"God damn you!" again.

I winced, till I realized from the voice's faintness that he hadn't come much closer than this side of the ditch, the gap in the fence, maybe the dirt pile. And I saw no sign of a flashlight. Still, he might be coming on yet, however slowly or clumsily. I couldn't stay long. I waited, breathed, till either I figured he was gone or until I couldn't stand it anymore—couldn't tell you which.

Minutes. No idea how many—I didn't dare open my cell

phone to see. But long enough that I had to pee, and did it, rolling sideways, into a little depression I'd felt in the dirt.

The pee smelled, I smelled, and it had to have been an hour. Slowly as I could—and that's pretty slow—I rose. Turned. And walked toward the yard. Couple of thousand bucks in gear be damned—I wasn't going back that way.

The container yard's main building loomed large. The cranes creaked and squealed, cables hummed, and containers banged ever louder.

What would I do? Waltz right into the container building? What would I get—a cheery greeting, a cup of cocoa and a comforting blanket, a ride to the main gate? Hell, I was filthy, head to toe, and bloodied here and there, my face included. Limping, too, I realized. No, there'd be trespassing charges and—

Still, I walked that line of sight Mac had mapped for me. I'd think of *something* before I got there.

It was right there before me. Hapag-Lloyd, right in line. Something-something-five-oh-six. Scrawled under the Lloyd name, in silver spray-paint, fresh enough it couldn't have been there more than days, three-six-gamma.

I stopped. Looked left. Squinted, wiped the wet out of my eyes. Way down the end. Trailer. Red letters across the rear doors. Crete.

I had to look. I'd earned the right. Felt better going this way anyhow. I'd seen figures moving about here and there on the container lot, though it seemed they hadn't seen me. Out on the trailer lot: Nothing. No one.

The ground leveled as I neared, the footing not so bad, now, the light a little better. Maybe I'd find a gap in the fence. Maybe, I thought wildly, walk over to the south gate, pass myself off as a worker at quitting time, one who'd got into some especially dirty business. Which, no doubt, I had, in more ways than one.

The Crete trailer neared. MacDonald's instructions. I dug my cell phone out of a pants pocket with a tear big enough I could have lost it. Lucky.

"MacDonald?"

"Yeah."

"Crete."

That, he'd told me, was all I'd need to say.

I heard some kind of sigh, some kind of letting-go of breath on the other end. Then: "Thank you, Jack. You can pack up and go home, now."

"Um…not exactly, Mac."

"Why not?"

"Tell you when you get here."

MacDonald sighed. I hung up.

I stood. Then heard. Movement, inside the trailer. Muffled sounds that *couldn't* be voices. Could they?

I closed my phone, found another pocket for it.

And in that pocket, found my folding Gerber.

I had to know. I flicked the Gerber open on my second try, discovering I'd lost some little piece of flesh from the end of my thumb. A little more blood, too. Got some on my face when I licked the thumb.

At the back of the trailer, I reached up, foot on the step, grabbed for a door hinge, missed, grabbed again and succeeded. Had to saw through the damn plastic seal—why did I never remember to sharpen that knife? Jumped down. Reached for the door lever, jerked it, pulled the right-hand door open.

The left opened by itself.

Flashlight from inside. Eyes. Mexicans, by the look of them. A dozen or more, maybe two.

Wildlife.

The flashlight turned on me.

Heavy accent, bit of a sneer: "You look like shit, mang."

17.

01 August, late morning
The Yellow-Breasted Corncrake

I wasn't going to just let that gear go. It wasn't Eileen's. Red Line didn't even own surveillance gear. As hard-boiled as they got was a little internet sneakery. No, I'd bought and paid for that stuff myself. Or Lynette had.

I made McDonald meet me at the grocery on Raines. To get even that much, I had to say *You owe me*. And *Bring my gun*.

He complied. Beyond that, all I got for my trouble was *You look even worse in the daylight*, my piece and holster perfunctorily handed to me in a paper lunch bag, and his refusal to accompany me to my no-longer-private little corner of the CN yard. He just shook his head. "Sorry. I can't risk being seen."

Then: "Look, I really am sorry. I owe you better, Jack. I'll explain, I will. Not now, but...just go get your..."

The look on my face told him there was little he could say. He sighed, turned, left.

I went to the indent in the fence, found the gate still unlocked, drove all the way in, walked over the ditch to my dirt pile, mumbling something between bitching and prayer that I'd find my gear. There was none of it left. Not so much as a dropped lens cap. I'd have to tell Mac: A couple of trips to the Chinese buffet wasn't going to cut it.

I did see a dog, an old, yellow, snarling thing, nosing the dirtied remains of what looked like a Snickers bar. Prints from my own combat boots. Another set of prints—mismatched shoes, one smaller, one larger, and running alongside those, the repeated imprint of a cane. And, on the plank bridge across the reeking ditch, a great spat gob of what had to be chaw.

That and two empty shotgun shells. Ten-gauge. Those I bagged and took away, figuring I'd give them to MacDonald.

Not that I carry all that CSI stuff around with me. But I did find on the dirt pile the empty baggie from one of my tuna sandwiches, so I tweaked the shells into that, using a pencil, resealed the baggie.

Evidence.

Of what, I didn't know.

18.

03 August, early afternoon
Nikki's Bedside Manner

"Cut yourself shaving, Jack?"

"Stuff it, toots."

"Free coffee and kiss it better?" Nikki said.

"Your coffee's crap. I'll take the kiss and an orange juice," I said.

"The hell you will," Nikki said. "Our orange juice has eight *kilo*grams of sugar a serving."

"And the company thinks there's forty-two servings in this," I said, hoisting the OJ I'd grabbed, setting it back in the rack.

"Sit your chubby little ass down," she said. "You look a mite stove up. Eileen take you two falls out of three? Or did Miz Mc-Corkle and you do some rasslin' last night?"

"I don't know I can get up again," I said. "Gonna bring me my coffee?"

"That 'n' more," she said.

True to her word, is our Nikki. Cappuccino in a china cup, napkins, the works, all as she stood before me. Skinny, she said, but still…and last, a kiss. Bent down and planted it right on the mouth. There's a first time for everything. I got a good look at the bruising. Still bad, a few more colours than the traditional black and blue. But she'd done a good job hiding the worst of it with some cream, blush, whatever all that stuff is. And the kiss wasn't bad.

"French cost extra, Nikki?"

"We're talking whole new tax bracket, bozo," she said, and moved back to the counter.

"Nikki," I said. "I wanted to ask you about—"

"No you don't," she said, reappearing. I thought I saw a subtle nod toward the door.

A sudden appearance. MacDonald. New suit. Blazing white shirt, English spread collar. Turquoise paisley tie and chewing a toothpick, leaning hands-in-pockets against the wall. "I *like* to watch," he said.

Fifteen minutes of cruel banter. Score: MacDonald, fifteen… Minyard, zero.

Then, seated, serious: "How much you know, Jack?"

"By 'wildlife,' you meant Mexicans," I said.

"Kinda," he said.

"Park that," I said. "We'll clear that up later. Three-six gamma."

"*Not* gang graffiti, Jack."

"I knew that." Which, sort of, I did. "Lining up, radio tower?"

"Low-tech signaling. Ingenious. They didn't touch cell phones," he said. "Stopped that weeks and weeks ago."

"Couldn't they have used burn phones?" I asked.

"Burn phones?" he said. "You get all this lingo from TV, don'tcha." He shook his head. "Caught two of them that way already. New technology. 'Sides, we had two of them nailed on the Mexican end. We turned both. One of them died in prison. The other—well, whereabouts unknown, now," he said. "But we got what we wanted out of him. So they turned to semaphore signals."

"Semaphore? Like in, Boy Scouts, waving flags?"

"Something like," he said. "They'd got hold of some guys from the trucking company—"

"Crete," you mean.

"Yup. Perfectly legitimate company. The company itself was clean as a whistle. But the cartel had got hold of three guys, truckers and a dispatcher, plus a yard guy from CN, another guy at the container pool. All had rap sheets, here and there, and somehow they'd got past HR at Crete and CN. Blackmail—said they'd spill the beans to the companies if they didn't go along. Some place of origin for the container, they'd get one with one of the right numbers, spray the graffiti on. Deal was—if the yard crane happened to drop the container in that exact position—"

"End of the row—"

"Yup. Position 14101—fourteenth rank, row one, bottom—then that meant the next night there'd be a shipment of prime Mexican beef—"

"*That's* a little cruel, Mac."

"You should meet the people into this kinda thing, Jack."

"I wonder whether I haven't."

"The guy who shot at you, Jack?" That wasn't, as it happens, who I'd been thinking of. But I didn't let on.

"Yeah, Mac. I tied him to the old house, the one behind."

MacDonald smiled, sat back, arms folded. "Do, please. Detect on, old chum..."

"So..." I leaned in. Got to filling in the rest of the story. No slouch of a P.I. here, no, sir. "That window on the top floor—that's where they observed from—"

"Uh-huh," he said, smiling.

"Then—" Things dawn on me slowly, sometimes. "Mac, you said, I see the container with the number and three-six-gamma, that's a sign the trailer with the Mexican illegals will appear the *next* night. But I only saw it the..."

MacDonald licked his finger, marked a '1' in the air. "That's because you skipped your duty the night of July thirtieth," he said. "Slacker."

"So I just happened to bump into this container when I ran over—"

"Yup," he said. "Thing had been sitting there twenty-four hours or more."

"And the Mexicans?"

"Been there about twenty minutes, Jack," he said. "So Crete's and the yard's records told us."

"So I got myself winded and carved up for noth—"

"No, no," he said. "Yard records wouldn't have picked out the container by number. What mattered was the combination of the container number and the graffiti. And that we could get only through visual observation."

"So I *wasn't* useless at—"

"Not at all," he said. "I'm grateful."

I went for broke. "Grateful enough to replace three thousand dollars' worth of surveillance equipment?"

"Um…grateful enough to *want* to…"

Sigh.

"So. Mac. The old house. The gang used the upstairs window to make the same observations I was doing?"

"Yup."

"And you caught—"

"Red-handed," he said. "Two guys."

"One of whom was the geezer with the cane and the shotgun."

"Um…no," he said. "As it happens."

"Well, who the hell is *he* in this crazy plot?"

"Best we can tell, Jack—the whole police force, I mean…he's just…some old geezer with a cane and a shotgun. Comes up, does this kinda stuff every six months or so, been doing it for a couple of years. Reports from all over South Memphis."

"So he didn't confess to—"

"No, Jack, you don't understand. We haven't *caught* him. We haven't any idea *who he is*."

"I did bag two of his shotgun shells for you, Mac."

"And thank you *so* much, sweetie, for helping Mommy make the cookies. Now go watch cartoons and Mommy clean up this mess."

"Couldn't you get any prints off the casings?" I asked.

"He's real careful," Mac said.

"DNA, I don't suppose?"

"DNA would be pretty slight, to begin with, Jack. Second, might not survive the blast of firing very well. Third, his DNA wouldn't get on the casings *after* firing—the shells'd likely just eject. Fourth...well, we did try to see what the lab could do, but..."

"But what, Mac?"

He reached into his suit jacket pocket. "Here's your Super Duper Official Junior CSI Kit, Jack," he said. Pair of latex gloves. Purpose-manufactured evidence bags with labels—not at all like the plastic sandwich baggie I'd improvised with. Official Memphis PD marker pen. "Next time," he said, "try your best not to get mayonnaise and tuna all over your evidence."

"So this geriatric nutcase," I said. "He's still out there?"

"Alive and not quite well, so far as we can tell," Mac said. "Perhaps you two'll meet one day."

"Christ, I hope—"

"Might turn out to be a nice old guy," he said. "I'm seeing the two of you together...rockers on the front porch...talkin' old times."

I heaved a resentful sigh and broke a smile at the same time.

"And if he's still luggin' the shotgun," he said, "maybe you can still outrun him."

19.

25 July, early afternoon
Collierville

If you think you're too classy for Memphis, Cordova, or Bartlett, you live in Germantown. Think you're too classy for Germantown, you live in Collierville, one burg farther out. Too classy for the planet, you live in Meadow Woods. Nominally, legally, administratively part of the city of Collierville, Meadow Woods drew a line, distinguishing itself. 'Now Entering Meadow Woods', said a brick-and-stone sign, ringed in meticulously maintained monkey-grass and blooming irises, a rig that couldn't have cost less than my annual income. Fitting—some of those lots were large enough they'd be a chore to walk across, and some you'd be tempted to drive. If Germantown had "gated communities," I thought, this one would have machine guns and concertina wire. All, of course, correctly landscaped.

Somewhere back at city hall, these houses had street numbers. Out here, though, they had names. *The Briars. Cotton Hill. Levee Reach.* Clayton McCorkle's *Winter Bayou*, I saw from the copied plat I'd scooped from Collierville's planning department, was the only number on its street. A street I'd not be driving, I saw. The iron gate would have looked formidable if I'd been driving a tank. How he'd scooped private possession of a whole city street for his own was anyone's guess. But, then, there's a lot goes on in Memphis that has to do with extraordinary privilege.

I hadn't come to see Barbara Jean, wasn't intending to go in. I just wanted to see the place for myself. And couldn't quite. Not from the gate, which gave a view of a curving rock wall and another inner gate. And security cams, on poles and trees—moving cams, I noted. I backed Mitzi out, guessing my picture had already been taken at the outer gate, looked for another viewpoint, and found it, finally, on the north side of the property, where some horticulturally horrific disease had evidently struck a stretch of hedge and left its limbs bereft of leaves. I parked, struggled up a rise, clambered to the top of the stone wall and over the crest of the rise where the wall ran lower than elsewhere. And, through the hedge's barren limbs, saw.

The house loomed out of the hilltop, about the size of an aircraft carrier. A house built less for its style than for its brute visual weight. Not necessarily handsome, architecturally. And certainly not what you'd call beautiful. Impressive, yes—in the way a gigantic warehouse is impressive, when you see one for the first time. Imagine a McMansion—the kind you see in GeeTown and Collierville. You know how they assemble those. A French farmhouse roof here, white columns there, over here three dormers, there an eyebrow window, now a gable. A dog's breakfast. "Architectonic," you might say—a borrowing from every period, movement, regional style, and every bit of it *faux*. Like an ignorant, angry kid who stole every Lego piece in town and all he wanted was to make whatever he was building *big*.

Clayton McCorkle had made it big. In construction, mostly—not surprising, given the acres of square-footage I was staring at. I'd scouted him out at the Crescent Club, on the say-so of a couple of buddies who hung about the fringes of local wealth. The fact McCorkle met people at the Crescent Club—three, four times a week, the bartender told me—said a lot. If you were old money, if you had pedigree, you'd more likely meet at the University Club in Midtown, where you'd still hear, straight-faced, the term *respectability*, in accents that harkened back to an imagined Old South. The kind of respectability, incidentally, that meant the only black people on the premises were "servants." And called that.

The Crescent Club, though, perched atop the building that lent its name, an elegantly anonymous late-eighties edifice that defined the east end of the Poplar-240 split. A building of vaguely styled "consultants," a building of new-money brokers who'd made it on new-money clients and therefore could sport golf shirts and sockless, open-toed sandals in the office—the grown-up, monied equivalent of Memphis State frat boys sporting backwards ball caps and thinking themselves original, defiant, their own men. The Crescent Club took anyone who could write the cheque—more modest than the term *private club* might make you think—and didn't actually smell. They'd even taken MacDonald, whose card I used at the door, my thumb over his picture.

Three times that week, I'd sat near Clayton McCorkle and his buddies—a breakfast and two lunches. No need for disguises or subterfuge—in a club, you'd expect to see the same people. I heard laughter. A couple of dirty crony-jokes. And a guy deeply into construction, construction people, and not much else. One day, he came in brushing dust off his khakis, which bore another, darker stain. "Guy on a site," he said to the trio who'd been waiting too long and decided they'd best get on with lunch. "Not mine—a subcontractor's guy. Half cut his thumb off with a skill-saw. I hadda take him to Collierville Baptist. Poor bastard got no insurance, so we're gonna take care of him." He sat, wrote the name out three times on his own business cards, handed them around. "Put this old boy in your prayers, y'all. Grace a God, nerves in his hand won't be all fucked up."

The Crescent Club was one thing. Clean. Air-conditioned. Safe. Out here at the house…I moved along the wall…

20.

27 July, afternoon
Teatime

"You buying?" MacDonald said through the phone.

"Yep," I said. "I'm expecting some money, so I thought I'd splurge. Big cheque from the Memphis PD for all that camera equipment."

"Sarcastic bastard," he said. "It's what? Four o'clock. Perfect for tea. Does Bucks have crumpets?"

"Kind of," I said. "Still British, Mac?"

"There'll always be an England."

"Shut up and get here," I said. "We're going to have a little chat."

"You and me, Jack?"

"We're two of the three," I said, and all I got back was "Oh."

MacDonald arrived, sat. "Nikki," I said. "Get someone else to take the counter and come over here."

"Jack, I can't just—"

"Do it," I said. The old platoon commander in me was talking again. And it worked. She sat, moved her chair oddly close to MacDonald's.

"Now, old buddy," MacDonald said. "Before we get into—"

"We are into it, Mac."

He looked at me, looked away. Nikki looked at Mac, got nothing back.

"Nikki, that was Mac you called the morning you were…"

She breathed, looked me in the eye. "I figured you knew."

"I'm slow on the uptake," I said. "But I get it sooner or later."

MacDonald sighed, exchanged a glance with Nikki. "We've been…*seeing* one another."

"'Seeing'?" I said. "Is *that* what they're calling it now—"

Mac shook his head. "We're…"

"We're just friends," Nikki said, and there wasn't a hint of defensiveness.

"Fact is, Jack, I never had a girl—"

"Woman," Nikki corrected, and he smiled. "I'm trying to convince this Neanderthal that some women possess grey matter beyond a brain stem and a set of nasty bits," she said.

"So you two have been talking, what—books?"

"Yes," said Mac with a touch of genuine indignation. "Literature and shit."

"I see," I said, hoping I was projecting a faint amusement. I felt my smile vanish as I added, "I'd like to talk about the 'and shit.'"

MacDonald breathed. Nikki breathed. I didn't.

Mac was about to speak, but Nikki broke the silence. "Jig's up, Mac."

"You. Nikki. You're the reason Nikki was…"

Nikki's face said, for the first time in days, she still felt the pain.

"Yes," MacDonald said. "My fault. Best I can figure was, this guy wanted to hurt me by hurting someone…close to me. Figure he'd seen us out somewhere, some restaurant—"

"We like Chinese," Nikki chimed in.

"New Nam King?" I asked.

"Ain't the best place, but it's..."

"Handy," she said, looking at him, turning back to me. "You know—for conversation..."

"And shit," I said.

"There isn't any of that, Jack," said Mac. "Not that it'd be *your* business."

"I'm sorry," I said, and it occurred: It wasn't my business.

"So who hit you?" I asked Nikki.

Mac filled it in. "We don't know. Got a half-assed description—"

"I gave you a *very* good description," Nikki intruded.

"Description, is all," Mac added, touching the back of Nikki's hand.

"Has to do with this whole 'commission' crap, doesn't it," I said. It wasn't a question, and MacDonald's silence said it needn't have been.

"We don't know who it was," Mac said, and Nikki shrugged.

The next move was mine. "I think I do."

I stuck to my word. Can't lie to a lady. Barbara Jean McCorkle had asked for my discretion, and I honoured that.

Somehow, MacDonald knew better than to ask.

21.

31 July, dusk
Collierville

I'd been following Clayton McCorkle steadily for three days now. A time or two to his real estate office, a few more times to the Crescent Club. Twice way along Summer Avenue—once to what turned out to be some stand-around cocktail thing at Rhodes College. The other time, I lost him not far from the Paris Cinema, where he turned off on a side street and I missed him, dumb enough to be in the wrong lane. But I knew who lived on that street.

I kept squeezing MacDonald for whatever I could. I didn't believe it all, and it was clear he was holding back. But still, he was far more forthcoming than usual. The 'commission,' of course, was bogus. Or half so. It was all off the books. "Personal," MacDonald said, between him and Mayor Wharton. Seems Wharton wasn't sure who he could count on, but he trusted Mac. *Someone*, Wharton knew, was dirty. Wharton had known Mac's family from back when, and that still counts for a lot in Memphis. Why Mac had said anything at all to *me*, given all this hush-hush, about his 'commission,' his 'task force,' was a mystery I'd get to later. Right now, I was sitting on Clayton McCorkle and His Eminence, drinking tepid Styrofoam coffee in the car, outside a Collierville restaurant I couldn't afford to walk into, let alone dine at.

When they came out, it was His Eminence I decided to follow. I wasn't sure, but I thought McCorkle glanced my way not once, but twice.

22.

04 August, just after sunset
Collierville

There are things you don't forget from infantry training. Whenever else you might sleep, it's a hundred per cent stand-to for a half hour before and after dawn, a half hour before and after sunset. The sky's still bright, but the ground is dark. It's hard to pick out movement on the ground. Prime time for planned attack, prime time for ambush.

I'd got over a low stretch of wall surrounding the McCorkle residence, though not without a rip in the thigh of a pair of pants too good to rip. Damn things never tear on a seam, always someplace you'll see the repair. Lynette had never believed in repairing things, though I was still darning socks when I met her. "You replace them," she'd said.

I'd talked to Mac that afternoon. He'd called me. Unusually forthcoming, he simply announced, "We got 'im."

"Who?"

"Booking sheet says 'Martavius Hooton.'"

"His Eminence?"

"Yup. A little less eminent than before."

"Guess he won't be delivering his Sunday sermon."

"Guess not."

"Hit the news yet, Mac? It's gonna be all *over* town."

"Ain't gonna, Jack. Not for a coupla days."

"You got him on ice?"

"Busy as our beleaguered police force is, Jack, it seems some paperwork has momentarily been misplaced, and the Right Reverend Hooton is currently residing with us in what you might call a…secure location."

"Not 201 Poplar, I take it."

"Oh, no, Jack. The commission has security arrangements of its own. Thanks to the cooperation of, shall we say, a not-so-nearby county."

"And the charges?"

"I suspect you know, Jack."

"I have an hypothesis or two."

"'An' hypothesis, Jack? Isn't that a little too English teacher, even for you?"

"Touché. Importing those Mexicans?"

"Yeah," he said, squeezing a shrug through the phone. "And then some."

"You mean sex trafficking. Girls from China, Phillipines."

"Figured you knew," he said.

"Figured you knew I knew."

"I think what you don't know is…three dead girls."

"Jesus," I said.

"You know, somehow, Jack, in all this fuss, I neglected to stick a GPS on your ass. Where you at?"

"About five minutes from Starbucks."

"Jack, when aren't you five minutes from Starbucks?"

"Fair point," I said.

"And where will you be tonight?"

"Actually, I have no particular plans for this evening, Mac. What do you have in mind?"

"It's not an invitation, Kemosabe. And you do most certainly have plans for tonight."

"I do indeed." And that's all I gave him.

I don't know why, but I kept playing the conversation over in my head as I squatted in one of the more unkempt hedges in this corner of the McCorkle property. Dusk gave way to dark, waiting to boredom. And boredom gave way to a set of earbuds and some Steely Dan. That oddly listenable Fagen whine. *Aja...when all my dime dancin' is through...*

The beginning of a headache. Eyes wanting to close. A figure, leaving the house. Maybe—too tired to be certain.

I wished Mac had stuck me with a GPS. The next thing I knew was: First light. Massive swelling on the right side of my face. Me, on my side, my whole left side covered in mud and leaves. Grinding pain. And a light, sweet drizzle in the brightening dawn.

23.

18 August, early afternoon
Breaking News

"Can you come down to my office?" MacDonald.

"Well, I could…"

"You must," he said.

"I would if I knew where your fricking office was, MacDonald."

"I'm sorry," he said. "I meant to call, I really did. But Jack—"

"You see this thing on the news?"

"*What* thing?"

Sounded to me like: *Yeah, I know*. So I called him on it.

A sigh filled the phone.

"I replaced him, Jack. So now I reckon you know where my God damn office is."

Not fifteen minutes before, Channel 5 had cut into whatever afternoon girl-TV I'd been watching. A cop, a major, Harold Formley, removed from his job in a big way. Press conference from Chief Larry, another from Mayor A.C. Wharton. Formley had been found with child porn on his office computer, of all things. Tucked away, he thought, behind some super-secret security wall. But he hadn't figured on a new secretary with a masters in computing science she hadn't mentioned on the job app. After the warrant, they found worse on his home computer. And pictures, printed, tucked in a briefcase he'd forgotten to take with him at the end of his shift. He'd been running protection for what had been called "parties." For "gentlemen." Gentlemen, that is, who *didn't* prefer blondes, didn't prefer the local pros, liked them exotic, liked them young. And, sometimes, liked it rough. Half a dozen cops on protection outside these parties—none, beyond Formley, named. Two lawyers, a couple of investment guys, and a lower-court judge, were the rumours, the TV said. No names there, either. Nothing known, they said, about the location of these parties. Except, vaguely, "the eastern part of the metro area."

The major having been marched out, the Union Avenue precinct needed a new boss. "Just interim," Mac said when I got there. "But still..."

"Sad," I said. "Friend of yours?"

"Met him," Mac said. "But friend? No. Still, one of our own..."

"Thank God for guys like you," I said. His face said the line had come across a little flat.

"Gets worse," he said.

"How much worse?"

"Wish I could tell you, Jack," he said. "You don't know how much I wish I could tell you."

"Lunch?" I said. "Might ease the pain."

"Sure, but..."

"What?"

"Um...I'm a bit embarrassed, but...they hauled me in here so fast...I forgot my wallet."

I shot him a Johnny Carson deadpan.

"I swear, Jack, I swear, I will make this up to you."

"Oh, you will," I said. "You will. Now. You like upscale places, don't you, Major MacDonald. Don't you?"

"I do indeed."

"Lovely. There's that Chick-Fil-A right across the street."

"You've mentioned that."

We settled on the Pho Saigon, and took my car. Mac threw his briefcase in the back seat. It was clear MacDonald wanted the conversation kept light, and had a whole lot, anyway, that he couldn't and wouldn't tell me. So light I kept it.

Back at the Union Avenue precinct, I pulled up by the front door. Mac hopped out, a perfunctory thanks, not much else to say. He jerked the handle on the back door. "Sorry!" I said, and rocked the lock button to open. He reached in for his briefcase.

"Christ," he said. "Christ almighty."

I put the car in park, turned. If a guy as brown as MacDonald can look pale, he did.

"This," he said.

He held up a copy of a copy. Eight by ten. I'd scooped one of the pictures Barbara Jean McCorkle had shown me, scooped it without her seeing. Made my own Xerox to tuck in a file. My file had spilled over the seat as I'd turned back onto Union. The little Filipina girl. The dress. So pretty.

"Park right here," he said. "You'll need to come into the office."

I did, querulous, clueless, following Mac as he and his briefcase and my file preceded.

"This hasn't hit the news yet," he said.

"What?"

"Dead," he said. "State Line Road, this morning."

He showed me the crime scene shots. Nothing pretty at all. Whoever had done this had wanted more than a dead girl. He'd wanted to send a message.

"How the hell did *you* get *her* picture? And where? And from whom?"

24.

Winter begins on Summer Avenue.

The Admiral Benbow Inn went under. Twice.

Once, late September. I popped home at noon, uncharacteristically, for a file I'd forgotten. Stuck my key card in the door. No green light, no nothing. But the door creaked open, just from my touch. "What?" a voice said, half a dozen doors down, as a woman I hadn't seen before made the same discovery on stepping up, card in hand, to her room.

The woman was as surprised as I. All I could manage was a dull *I don't know*. My stuff was all there, untouched. I went inside, to the office, looking for Mrs. Patel. Admiral Benbow is closed, said a hand-scrawled sign taped to the window of the cashier's cage. Call owner. And a number with an area code I didn't recognize. It was disconnected anyway. I packed up and loaded my car—an hour, still hot, tore my pants on a nail in the door jamb. Went to some anonymous place in that clutch of fading motels of the 240 at Sycamore View, and bought a week, in cash. I stayed two, went to some other place. Never really unloaded the car—just the clothes I needed, a few favourite books, and my stamp albums. Neither one of the places had the feel of home—not like the Benbow.

Second time, late October. Driving by, hadn't been that way in a week or more. The Benbow had gone under again—literally, this time. Buildings razed, plowed under, all bulldozed, even the pavement of the lot. Couple of gigantic dumpsters. Most of the lot remained barren, plantless, save for a lone, idiot tree in a last remaining flowerbed, just inside the iron fence. Where the pool had been, though, grass had grown, unusually lush and green.

The sign still stood, near where the lobby had been. The name was gone, but the powerless neon outline of the admiral's tricorn hat remained. And, on the marquee below, some last, imperfect act by the last employee to leave, one of the stick-on letters having fallen, a misbegotten but apt attempt at a past participle:

losed.

My last prescription of Thorazine ran out. I'm not sure how long ago. Weeks, anyway. An embarrassed moment at the Kroger pharmacy—*No, no, check again, I'm sure there's one more refill*...I left after quite a little hissy-fit. Stayed up all night watching a marathon run of those programs—extreme asses killing themselves jumping off roofs on rollerblades, that kind of crap. Played with my stamps till dawn.

I know Doctor Nigeria would have written me another scrip. But I just—what with one thing and another—never did ask. He smiled, said he liked the fact I'd taken in my belt a notch.

I've moved again. Back on Summer. The other side of the 240, the east side, quite a bit closer to Eileen's office, where I seem to be spending rather more time, now, on rather more cases.

The Guest Inn—such a *generic*-sounding name—has a *somewhat* nicer lobby. Coffee's decent. Big cups. Sir sticks. All the Splenda you could want. They put out apples and bananas. Milk, too. I've become quite a milk drinker—I like a nice cold glass after my morning walk, right before I hit the AA meeting in the old Korean Baptist Church. Make-your-own waffles, too. But I've learned to leave them alone.

They have a sufficient variety of insect life, the Guest Inn— enough to amuse an entomologist or a twelve-year-old. And they also feature hot and cold running hookers. But most of both are confined to the other wing, the old and not so nice wing, far side of the pool. Which, incidentally, is blue. Or clear. Depending on how you look at it. And, now well past the season, closed. I was out there, mind you, the other night, poolside, lying in a chaise longue, alternating between reading the star map by flashlight in the centrefold of the November *Sky and Telescope* and trying to find the Orion nebula through binoculars and the soup that Memphis calls a sky. New binoculars, incidentally. A gift from MacDonald. Biggies, too—eighty mil, ten-to-twenty zoom. Zeiss, no less. He's on this German kick, now.

Bucks is still there, way down Summer. And Nikki, too. Lippy as ever, visibly ticked at the days I don't come in. She had no end of smartass comments about my face—as long as the bruising showed. And an act or two of kindness, as well.

One morning, I stopped in at the Union Avenue Starbucks, stood in line after setting up my laptop at the community table. A voice behind me said, "Will you let me buy your coffee, Mr. Minyard?" Unmistakable. I'd seen him a few times here before, met him once, years ago. I was sure he wouldn't remember. Not only did Mayor Wharton buy, but he sat with me. Briefly, at least. He said little—just pleasantries. He smiled, slid an envelope across the table, and took his leave. "Thanks," he said from the door. I opened the envelope: three thousand dollars—cash.

I got a one-up on MacDonald—he hadn't caught on to Clayton McCorkle. But he had excuses, as usual. "Geez, Jack," he'd said. "It was a one-man investigation."

"One and a half," I'd said back quietly. But I filled him in. The trouble: McCorkle was missing, and there was no credit card trail.

Friday last, I had that date with Jackie. Quite unexpected. Her idea, too. Out of the blue. Early movie and a quiet dinner out. Separate cars—we met at Starbucks and picked the movie out of the paper. She showed up in black spandex jeans, white blouse, a black blazer, and a smile. "The jeans are Eileen's idea," she said. "Haven't had them out in years, but she said you'd like the look." Just a hug when we left the restaurant—no big thing. But we'd talked a long time, longer than either of us knew, and I learned she liked Scrabble and had once belonged to the Memphis Astronomical Society and hoped to finish her BA—in English. She liked wearing those jeans, she said, liked the way they made her feel. She kissed me on the cheek and whispered, "I have these in two more colours. Free next Friday?"

I've been receiving tailor-made dress shirts in the mail. From Thailand. "But they're British *style*," MacDonald says. And a couple of luridly European ties, definitely *not* from Thailand. Or eBay.

Red Line's looking for a real P.I. now, a no-pretend employee—they're branching out. "No promises," Eileen said yesterday. And she insisted on putting an ad in the paper. "It's the thing to do. Protocol, you know." She looked at me, dead cold. Smiled. Handed me an envelope. "But this might improve your chances." Inside, unsolicited, a five-thousand-dollar bonus cheque, on the Dwayne Poteat case, from Giant Bloodsucking Insurance Group of America, made out directly to me. Some veepee even wrote a note on her own stationery: *Jack…Thanks for the photo of the year!*

The Guest Inn has a new manager now. Met him Monday. Guy with a smile. "We are repaving, you are please parking over there, one veek only." His badge read: Mr. Patel. I had to ask. "No," he said. "Many Patel. Many many. You park there, please, one veek."

On a wider front, Barbara Jean McCorkle seems to have escaped the net. The FBI's not talking. Nor INS. Nor Homeland Security. MacDonald's on the whatsit-commission for real now, he tells me, but claims he's out of the loop on that specific subject. He means, of course, he's just not talking. But the TV news this morning said Interpol's looking for Barbara Jean somewhere in eastern Europe. Where the girls in the pictures have gone, those of them still alive, is anybody's guess.

In more local news there's this...I have not had a drink, now, in 447 days, by the grace of God, one damn day at a time. Mitzi will definitely need a new radiator, two new tires at least. But I think I can deal with that. I've finally bagged that bill stamp I've been looking for—the eight-cent first-issue blue, feather-in-the-bun, in a nice, bright block of four—mint, full gum, never hinged. And I heard a few minutes ago by phone, from MacDonald himself: Down on Mount Moriah, just an hour ago, Clayton McCorkle, alone in his room at the Marriott, dead.

Somewhere, they tell me, Jesus weeps. I haven't seen it myself. And even in the dark and the quiet, I haven't quite heard. But for no reason I can fathom, I still believe.

Acknowledgements

To those who, in various times and ways, have taught me writing or encouraged that writing: Guy Bailey, Shelley Baur, John Bensko, David Carson, Jamie Clarke, Teresa Dalle, Rick DeMarinis, Adrienne Devine, Charles Hall, Donald Hays, Al Heinreich, Barry Isaac, David H. Kelley, Jim Kelly, Stephen Malin, Jo McDougall, Kai Nielsen, Rosemary Nixon, Gordon Osing, Gene Plunka, Jim Rendall, Tom Russell, Brett Singer, Bruce Speck, Charles Stagg, Aritha Van Herk, Bill Washburn, Miller Williams.

To manager Kisan Patel and the staff of Panera Bread #4604, Germantown, Tennessee, and Scott Shellhart and the staff of Panera Bread #4602, Memphis, who have fueled this and so much other writing, endured so much of me.

To Kris Clinton, Blue Line Investigations LLC, of Bartlett, Tennessee, and to Marti Miller, private investigator, Memphis.

To the girls: Leah Bailey, Mary Berni, Kristin C, Megan Conti, Trish Fritsche, Liane Limport, Connie McConnaha, Linda M, Janet Pink, Julia Roa, Debbie Smith, Donna Tingley.

To artist-friends Les Linfoot, Angela Hoehn, Glenda Brown, who have taught me much about the connections between paint and words.

To Tony Branson, my fine friend, my own private Idahoan. And Sandy Branson.

To the members of Toastmasters International, and many Toastmasters friends across the world, all of whom help me believe.

To Holly Schmidt—artist, conversationalist, inspiration, friend, and a MENSA man's dream-date.

To my editorial clients and writing students, who keep my pen sharp. Thank you, especially, to those of my clients—Jim Paavola, Nancy Roe, Bill Townsend, Tonya Zavasta significantly among these—who have the jam to try their hands at fiction, the determination to dedicate themselves to learning craft, and the unseemly nerve to chafe at some of their editor's suggestions.

To friends, old and new…Craig Cope, Norma Duke, Ingrid Enns, Bill and Leslie Garries, Doug Levis, Gary K. Lowe, Charlotte Stokes, Tim Yip.

Most especially to my beloved wife, Elizabeth Deeley, for love and patience and friendship of a quite extraordinary order.

And, as a cavalier afterthought, to my bitch-goddess and perpetual muse, Peg Oneil, always the faithful fan, friend, encourager, and a disturbingly accurate critical reader. I know you never did like this text, Peg. You never did wear those boots for me, either. And now, you'll pretty much have to do both.